TALLADEGA NIGHTMARES

From the Files of the BSI

Book Seven

MARK EVERETT STONE

CAMEL PRESS

Kenmore, WA

For more information go to: www.camelpress.com
www.markeverettstone.com

Cover design by Jeanne Gustafson

Talladega Nightmares
Copyright © 2019 by Mark Everett Stone

ISBN: 9781603812580 (Trade Paper)
ISBN: 9781603812597 (eBook)

Library of Congress Control Number: 2018958008

Produced in the United States of America

To all of you who enjoyed the adventures of Kal and Canton, thank you. Your feedback and enthusiasm made it all worthwhile.

CONTENTS

CONTENTS

PROLOGUE

———•———

"**D**O YOU THINK HE can hear us?"

"Nah. He's out cold. The sodium pentothal will keep him in the dark until after transition phase one." Clicking sounds and a soft hiss. Perhaps steam?

"How far back are we to send him?"

"Far enough. Just let me punch in the coordinates ... and there! All done. Transition in one minute."

"Jesus, that far? He must really be something to deserve this kind of vengeance."

"Don't mess with the bosses, let this be a lesson."

"If he's lucky his body won't be ripped into its component atoms and scattered across the universe."

"Nah, this tech is proven. He'll be fine. Too bad it's a one-way trip though. Makes it rather useless for the here and now. The only thing he'll have to worry about is temporal/spacial rifting due to quantum interference from his modern body, but the risk is small. Doesn't matter, though because once he's gone, he's gone."

"Charging Primary."

"Check."

"Set phase correction."

"Done."

"Ready?"

"And willing."

"Let's send this poor bastard …"

***

Fur and the smell of unwashed bodies, a whole heap of them and then some. Beneath the fried chicken smell of old sweat there was something else, something I sure knew down to my bones. The smell of blood and rot … and beneath that … the sea?

Heat next to me, a pervasive warmth all along my side. I turned my head to see a black mop of hair and the soft curve of lips. A woman by the feel. *What the hell*?

I disengaged and rolled over, realizing that the fur smell was actual fur, what looked like the pelts of several wolves sewn together to make a blanket. When I made it to my feet, moving quietly so as not to wake the woman, I saw that I was naked as the day I was born.

"What the …?" my mouth clamped shut of its own accord, my teeth clacking together hard enough to hurt my jaw. I was about to say Hell, but the word wouldn't come, only dry air.

My head hurt, a low thrumming pain that started behind my eyeballs and made its merry way to the back of my skull, but the rest of me seemed fine … fine enough that I could ignore my headache and take a gander at what lay all around.

A tent. Thick waxed canvass supported by an oak pole some four inches across. There was enough light coming through the canvas to hurt my sleep adjusted eyes. Furs on the ground and in one corner of the squarish tent lay a trunk only a little smaller than a footlocker, but made entirely of wood except for the hinges, which were iron. On top was a short sword with only the barest hint of a cross guard and leaning up against the trunk a large shield about three-feet long and two wide. Behind the trunk stood a spear that leaned against the wall, dimpling the canvas slightly against the nine-inch leaf-shaped blade.

"Is my lord happy?"

I whirled, startled. The woman was sitting up, full bare breasts hanging over the wolfskin blanket. I did me some gaping and gawking. Been a while since I beheld some feminine charms.

She smiled coyly, arching her back so I could get a better view. I felt myself stirring and I thought about football. Yeah, football … that's the ticket. "Was my lord happy with my performance? Would my lord like a repeat?"

Repeat? I didn't remember the first time, more's the pity. Since she wanted me to look, look I did. Pretty in a harsh sort of way, her brown eyes beckoned, but seemed a little wary as well and it took me a moment to realize that beneath all that hardness, wearing tough times like a second skin, was a young woman. Much younger than my four decades, although she had some country miles on her. "How old are you?" I asked.

Her smile faltered. "My lord captured me as his spoils, as is his right, when I was but twelve. Now I'm sixteen summers, but my lord already knows this."

Spoils? Captured? Sixteen? My balls wanted to creep up into my torso in shame. I diddled a sixteen-year-old girl last night? Stomach clenching, I turned away, suddenly ashamed of my nudity. My mamma woulda boxed my ears for a month of Sundays if she found out. I faced monsters, demi-gods, Sidhe and even púca with pointed sticks, but never a minor in my bed. Even one with a bodacious bod like she was sporting. My brain started to disconnect, warning lights and whistles flashing in my mind. Houston, we have a problem …

I am so going to hell, was my second thought. "A drink," I croaked, back to the woman. Girl. "I need a drink."

Shuffling noises then the sound of water splashing. Small, work-calloused hands thrust a cup into mine. I drank greedily.

And nearly spit it out. "What in the name of all that's holy is that?"

"Wine, my lord." The woman … girl, had to remember that. Girl, girl, girl. "Although unwatered, so it's strong. You don't like it? It's the finest *chian* available, I just opened the amphora, so it's fresh."

Strong? Fresh? Tasted like saltwater and Formula 409 and sugar and a host of other things that didn't belong in a fermented grape beverage. "What about water? Do we have water?"

"Ah, you need to bathe, my lord?"

"To drink." Although I was pretty ripe. Probably turn the bathwater black.

"My lord!" The woman. Girl dammit! "Drinking plain water by itself can cause the bowels to erupt! Surely you don't want that?"

No, I don't and please don't call me Shirley. And stop calling me 'My Lord'. It's starting to creep me out.

What the Sam Hill was going on around here? Where was I? "Where ... ah ... my mind is still sleep fuzzed and I can't seem to think straight."

Small hands stroked my long hair. "Oh, my lord, did you take a knock on the head during the last battle?"

Long hair? Couldn't be ... my hair was short all around, not because I liked it that way, but when you're in the thick of it, long hair gives a Supernatural something to hold onto before it starts eating your eyeballs for lunch. I ran my fingers through my hair. Yep, felt like mine. I closed my eyes to settle the sudden nausea in my stomach. Wait, didn't she mention something about a battle and a knock on the head?

Oh ... oh! Fortunately, Quantum Leap reruns prepared me for this. What would Sam Beckett do? "Uh, yes?"

The girl turned me around, so I could stare down into her dark, unfathomable eyes. My disconnect was threatening to derail my brain altogether and shove them out my ears. I became acutely aware of our nudity and the heat that flowed like a river between us, connecting us and I felt ...

Baseball, hockey, dead puppies ... we don't think of under-age girls ...

I was put squarely in the middle of crap creek without a

paddle or a clue. Wait … maybe one clue. Those voices, the ones that were conversing while I slept. What did that one say again … 'temporal/special rifting due to quantum interference from his modern body'. What did that mean?

It hit me, all at once, as the girl said, "You are my lord, Cantoneades, prince and cousin to King Diomedes of Argos. You are a great warrior, one of the great heroes of the Argives who have come to make war against the people of Ilios." Her hand stroked my long hair.

Those names. Familiar. They tickled my memory bump, but I couldn't force them to come because every time I reached for them, they slipped away like smoke on the wind, but they didn't relate to me. My name was Canton Alsate, Mescalero Apache and member of the BSI, not somebody's cousin from a place called Argos.

More disconnect, those big brown eyes that I could drown myself in spun out of my sight, but I was an agent trained to handle stressful situations and comport myself with the dignity and diligence expected of a representative of the United States government. We had plenty of shrinks in the Bureau who gave all good little foot soldiers tips on how to center ourselves.

Breathe in … breathe out. One, two, three, four, fivesix-seveneightnineten. All will be well. You're one bad mother, Canton Alsate, and the Creator hasn't made anything I can't handle.

When I was sure the tent stopped spinning, I had my answer. I knew where I was, and it left in my gut a gaping void like the heart of a collapsing star.

Without a word I turned and unlaced the tent flap, exiting into the light of day and what hit my eyes was pretty much what I expected.

Long, sandy beach, churned with blood and horse drop-pings and littered with multi-colored tents of all sizes. The beach must've stretched for over a mile and every square inch was covered, utilized by the army that camped there. Down by the water, hundreds of ancient wooden ships lay beached while out in the distance, about a half-mile away, hundreds more lay at anchor.

I turned and walked toward the rough wooden palisade that guarded the shoreline. It looked to be made of graying wood that seemed like it belonged elsewhere. A haphazard collection of planks that had seen better days. A rickety tower every fifty feet held a pair of men in armor, solid bronze breastplates, horsehair crested helmets and leaf-bladed spears. Wicked looking short swords were belted at their waists along with their studded leather kilts. I spotted a small gate and trundled my way, grunting, through the sand until I reached it.

"Where are you going, my lord?" If the soldiers atop the nearest wall were freaked out at my bare ass with my kibbles and bits hanging out, they didn't show it. Besides, it looked like plenty of the men on the beach were lounging *au naturale* themselves. Definitely warm enough for it. "You should set to armor if you want to gaze at the city."

I shook my head, sliding the gate bar to one side and walking through.

"My lord!"

I couldn't talk. My tongue was Krazy glued to the roof my mouth. Stretching before me was a flat plain that might have, at one point in the distant past, been green and lush, but not a blade of grass, no tree, nothing above the level of bacteria that could be called life remained. The ground was a tumbled mash of mud the color of old rust. A half mile away a sluggish, shallow river cut through the landscape, a brown flow that looked like it needed a date with a waste treatment plant.

It wasn't the dead plain, or the dirty river that affected me the most … it was the smell. It hit me in the face like a garbage truck at full speed. Here I thought a horde of naked and near naked people with questionable hygiene had odor. Not even close. What wafted off of that plain made my eyes water and my gag reflex kick into overdrive. For a few moments, all I could do was try not to throw up and wipe my eyes.

"Damn," I gagged. "Oh, double doggone dammit."

All the gagging and the tears hid the real sight from me, the thing that about dropped me like a slaughterhouse steer, the thing that stole my breath (which was darn lucky because I didn't want to do much breathing right about then) and left a hollow place where my heart used to be.

It was the city. The great, big city on a great big hill with great big goddamn walls that dominated the countryside from a good mile away. My dad runs construction, one of the biggest firms on the east coast and I knew enough about it to guestimate that those doggone walls topped out at fifty feet at the minimum. Rising above those walls were towers that wavered in the heat shimmer coming off the plain.

Oh, Christ on a cracker. I knew that city, not from sight, but from story, knew it because of the river, the plain of blood, the wall and the words Argives and Diomedes read in a half-remembered book when I was nineteen. I felt sick.

Somebody put me in the middle of the Trojan War.

CHAPTER ONE

Kal

———◆———

Strange Daze

OH LORD BUT ST. Louis really chapped my ass. As ops went, it was one of those that stick in the craw so hard it hurt like a chicken bone in the throat, but we saved the world as we know it from ending in an orgy of violence and screaming. The Angel of Mass Murder was what it called itself, that Supernatural who claimed the Quint Building and nearly the world. I was happy to see the end of him, but what I wasn't prepared for was the social media furor over the whole sorry mess.

Now that the world knows about Supernaturals and the BSI, everything we did that wasn't classified as Top Secret was fodder for the masses. The modern-day version of a Roman *Circus Maximus*. As long as the public had its bread and reality television, all was right in the world and we agents could continue throwing our bodies at the horrors that bleed in from the World Under, the dimension of monsters.

"You all right, love?" My wife's voice slid along my skin like silk as she twirled a finger in my mop of blond hair. Dark chocolate skin, a body so nice it made you believe in a loving god and a face that could make angels weep, Jeanie Hakala, nee Morrow, was far too good for the likes of this old Finnish boy. A magician in the Bureau, she had enough magical firepower, and the brains to back it up, to ensure she would always be employed at a ridiculous government salary. She was part of Special Branch, the R&D for the Bureau, the ones who came up with all the magical and tech geegaws that kept schlubs like me safe. When they worked. If they didn't, then someone got scraped off the walls.

"Turns out I have more Twitter followers than Canada has citizens," I said idly as I stared at my Bureau-issued smart-phone. "This is so weird."

Lips nibbled at an earlobe, which made my body react in the most interesting ways. "Who cares?" she murmured hot in my ear.

Go time. My own lips found hers for a serious Scandinavian lip lock and the room started to get a trifle warm as bits of clothing started to fly. Being with Jeanie was my tonic, a balm for the itch of the Bureau. Like an addict, I needed the BSI, but, like many of them, I hated what it turned me into, the erosion of my soul over the years. Oh, I did some good, saved the world a few times. All for the right reasons, but enough pain, violence and death takes a toll and it was Jeanie who kept me sane.

When I was fifteen my sister died rather violently at the hands (or tentacles) of a Finnish demi-god named Iku-Turso and her soul latched onto mine. She kept my mind from flying apart and gave me some serious optional extras like super strength and speed on tap, but, thankfully, her soul departed to a better place and the only thing that kept my fragile sanity whole was Jeanie and my little boy, Des.

So, when the opportunity arises for some horizontal nasty, I take it with both hands and don't look back. In this business you never know when the next Supernatural you meet might be your last.

"*Attention Agent Hakala,*" Andrea, BB's Receptionist

droned from the bone induction patch placed behind my left ear. *"Please report to Director Bauer's office immediately."*

Fantastic.

"You have got to be kidding me!" I blurted, tearing my lips away from some round and soft bits. "How does he know?"

Jeanie sighed and ran a hand along my cheek. She knew the score, but some day her near endless bounty of patience would run out and BB, my boss, would be on the wrong end of a feminine crapstorm. "Probably has the place bugged."

I looked around the small apartment reserved for agents on active duty. Two small rooms, bedroom and bathroom, well-appointed, luxurious despite the size. One thing about the Bureau, they expect the best, so they provide the best. "Wouldn't surprise me," I grumped. "But it's not his style."

My wife slapped my behind as I stood, and I gave her one last hot, lingering kiss before hightailing to BB's office.

Since the Bureau was now public knowledge and the digs were brand-spanking new, security to get to the director had been tightened to the point that it would take a tactical nuke to reach BB in his lair. Only POTUS, VPOTUS, and the Committee had the passwords, the rest of us just had to hope that BB wasn't in a bad mood when we walked down the long hallway to his office.

As usual, Andrea sat behind her desk, BB's last, best defense against intrusion. Used to be she'd have her hand on a sawed-off shotgun loaded with silver deer slugs fixed to a swivel under her desk, but nowadays all she had to do to defend against a hostile intruder was to press a small button. BAD THINGS would commence and said hostile would be swept up and placed in the nearest garbage bin. Don't kid yourself, though ... she still had the shotgun.

After Andrea made sure I wasn't some evil Doppelganger or malicious android sent by Klingons or some such, I strolled into BB's office. Still big like aircraft hangars are big, with sound-dampening dark blue short shag and a desk that, in reality, was actually one of the most powerful computers on the planet, so advanced I thought it might have been sent here by SKYNET. HAL 9000 would have proposed to that desk.

Benjamin Bauer, BB, my boss, sat on an obscenely overstuffed office chair with his hands behind his head and a beatific smile on his face.

Holy cats!

Was this a sign of the Apocalypse? Wile E. Coyote couldn't smile any wider than BB did right then. It was *terrifying*. I needed to get the hell out of there before Romulans arrived with disruptors firing for my tender bod.

"Relax, Kal." BB's voice was smooth silk and chocolate. He sounded happy, so happy that I was set for a major league freak out. His next words failed to comfort. "Nothing bad is going to happen."

"Says you!" I was starting to panic.

"Says me," he agreed. Still kept that damn creepy, happy smile on his face though. My skin wanted to crawl off my body and hide under the wet bar against the wall. BB gestured to the only other chair in the room, an uncomfortable looking wood and fabric conglomeration that seemed like it was made to cause hemorrhoids. I sat. Yep, as uncomfortable as it looked. I always thought BB was a closet sadist.

"You look disheveled," he said, still smiling. I hoped and prayed he'd *stop* that. "Did I interrupt anything?"

"My mellow. Right now, I'm about three seconds from running away screaming my bloody head off. C'mon, BB, chill me out before I have an aneurism." If I was lucky my head would *sploosh* all over the place like a scene from a bad horror flick and I'd be spared the terror.

Then he really peed in my Wheaties by saying, "I'm retiring." And the smile grew wider.

"Go [DELETED] yourself you're retiring!" Not my best comeback, but realize I was out of my depth here and frantically flailing.

Still that terrifying smile didn't waver an inch.

"Yes, in a few days I will be officially retired from government service. You won't have old BB to kick around anymore. Time to travel with the wife."

This just kept getting weirder and weirder. "You're married?"

"Yes."

"Since when?"

"Since 'I Do'. "

Now he was throwing snark right back at me. Me! Capt. Sarcastic of the Snark Express. I sat there with my mouth open wider than a politician's pockets. I half expected to hear the theme from *The Twilight Zone*.

"Shut your mouth, Kal, you're catching flies." BB sat further back in the chair and, if anything, his smile became more beatific. "Everything I've worked for, struggled and sweated for, has finally come to pass and now I can enjoy my life."

"Ubba dooba dieeba do."

He raised an eyebrow. "What?"

"You weren't making any sense," I said. "So, I decided to go for gibberish myself."

"Rein in your incoherence, Kal."

"Then catch me up."

"What do you think I've been doing these past years."

That was easy, but I had a sense it was a trick question. "Running the Bureau?" I half-asked, half-stated.

"Only a small fraction of my efforts."

"Okay, what's the big fraction then?"

"Trying to achieve what I have just achieved."

I smelled the odor of decay in Denmark, but curiosity had me asking, "And what is that?" The bottle of Stoly in at the wet bar looked pretty darn good, enough that my throat ached for the slow burn of vodka, but I'd been dry for over a year. Jeanie wouldn't throw a fit or anything, but the look of disappointment on her face when she found out would gut me. She had an unnerving habit of peeling back all my secrets.

It's a female conspiracy, I tell ya!

BB sighed but didn't lose his unnerving smile. "Do you know what it takes to run this place on a long-term basis?"

"I actually do *not* know that at all." Ah, the truth will set you free.

"Trust me you will. You're my replacement."

The truth sucks the big one.

Perhaps I blacked out for a few moments because when I regained some sort of sense there was a large tumbler of heavenly liquor at my lips and I was drinking greedily. After a couple of seconds, I realized I was standing at the wet bar slogging enough vodka to marinate my kidneys for a BBQ.

"What the [DELETED]?" I murmured. Where was I? What happened? My legs felt like soft rubber and a slow heat spread throughout my torso.

Long slow laughter answered me. BB was *laughing*!

End of days, dude. End of days.

"I thought you gave up drinking." My boss still sat in the obscenely comfortable looking office chair and, if anything, his grin was wider. It's like I was dropped in the Bizarro BSI.

"Sorry." I coughed. Too much Stoly too quickly. "Could have sworn you said I was replacing you as Director." Pshaw … no way. Must have been hallucinating.

"I did."

Reality hit the brakes for a second time as another shot of vodka hit my stomach at warp speed. I really needed a tribble to help me achieve a good mellow because I swear my blood pressure spiked to 245 and showed no signs of stopping there. Maybe my head would do me a favor and explode. Yeah, explode, good times.

"I am not going to allow your head to explode," BB said, easily reading my mind. "That would defeat the purpose of you becoming Director."

"But … how … when … I thought POTUS appointed …" Me and my silver tongue. If I were any smoother you could spread me on toast.

"Sit."

I left the bottle. Seemed the thing to do since I downed most of in a matter of a minute or so. Jeanie was going to be executively pissed. When my back cheeks hit the chair, I settled in, trying to get comfy, but had a feeling that wasn't going to happen for about three decades or so.

"When I first took the job as Director," BB began, still *smiling*, "I knew things had to change. Since its inception, the Bureau has been trampling the inalienable rights of its citizens without a worry about the consequences because, for the Bureau, there were none. I know you know all this, but there is one fact kept from the agents, one little tidbit of information not disseminated because of how alarming it is and what I'm about to tell you won't leave this room. You'll understand in a sec."

My head in my hands, voice muffled. "Oh, please don't."

No good. He told me. "The Interdiction isn't perfect, Kal. If you try to push it too hard, it'll eventually kill you."

What?

"I can tell by the mouth-agape look of shock on your face you can't quite process this, so let me explain slowly. Before the nineties, Interdiction was hardly used. Cellphones were still in their infancy and not everyone carried a digital camera. It was far easier to control and contain the narrative when a Supernatural outbreak occurred, but now everything is captured by cell phones and virtually everyone has one, so interdiction became the rule rather than exception.

"Because we monitor everyone with an Interdiction, we noticed that many of those Interdicted died suddenly and always of the same cause. An aneurysm. Blood vessels in their brains would literally explode in what's called Cerebrovascular Accident, or CVA. It didn't take long for Special Branch to find out the cause ... increasing strain against the Interdiction, people trying the hardest they could to circumvent the spell and convey the truth about the Bureau. Eventually the Interdiction killed them. Not the purpose of the spell, but a side effect, like you see in pharmaceutical commercials.

"When this danger came to my attention, I knew the old way of doing things had to stop. The public had a right to know about the World Under because we were using more and more Interdictions and, knowing how plain stubborn most people are, more deaths. This was about your sixth year in when you were considering ending your contract and retiring."

The warmth in my gut became a big greasy ball. What came next turned that greasy ball into a greasy lead weight.

"Do you remember the dinner we had in downtown D.C. a few years ago? That fancy sushi restaurant?"

I nodded. Acid burned the back of my throat.

"Remember what I said after our third cup of melon sake?"

Yeah, it was coming back. I nodded.

"You told me you wanted to retire, to try to bag Iku-Turso on your own because you thought you had a fix on him, reports of a Lovecraftian creature seen in the Indian Ocean."

Lovecraftian, what a term. Bureau legend had it that a young H.P. saw Iku-Turso in Greenwich Bay and it messed him up for life. His brilliant mind couldn't cope with what he saw. His sanity cracked like an egg dropped on concrete. There are artist renderings of Iku-Turso. All of them nightmare inducing, but they paled compared to the real deal. Imagine what seeing the real deal would do.

Sure, Lovecraft became the father of modern horror, but at what cost? Dead at forty-six. Me, I wanted to be run over by a semi-truck when I was one-hundred and two after making vigorous love to my wife.

Is that too much to ask?

The dinner, the sushi and the sake all came back. I wanted to burn every one of Iku-Turso's tentacles off and eat them like calamari. Revenge for him/it murdering my sister. I had a bead on him ... the Indian Ocean and I was rich enough to hire a goodly sized ship and enough armaments to conquer Africa. The clink of porcelain and the smell of tempura and fish, the strong, almost acidic taste of sake on my tongue. BB telling me in a low voice that it was impossible to bag the demi-god without Bureau assistance (turned out he was wrong) and that if I stayed in, he would do what he could to help. In the end, a few years later, he let me have my head and I hunted and banished Iku-Turso back to the World Under, and, afterward, returned to the Bureau.

"You convinced me to stay." I could hardly say the words.

"I needed you to stay. Your operations tended to be big and splashy. Somehow you seem *drawn* to those types of situations, as if the universe has decided that you receive all the most dangerous ops and I needed that to happen. I needed big, splashy, dangerous Kal Hakala to take on the big ones so more and more and more evidence of the World Under came to light, like it did in San Francisco. From then on it was only a matter of time before POTUS and all the other world leaders informed the public of the World Under."

"You wanted it all out?"

"I wanted to save lives, like I swore to do. I wanted to give the people a glimpse of the truth. They needed to see it before it exploded all over the world stage. I also wanted to restore a measure of power to the people because that's what this government is supposed to be … a government for the people, not for shadow organizations." BB's smile faded at the edges. "The results were better than I could have dreamed of. Civilization has stabilized, the truth is out there, and we are more effective by a factor of ten at containing incursions. No more willy-nilly trampling on civil rights because we can, or have to … there is accountability now. No more people dying from Interdiction and *no more goddamn hiding*." This last was a shout, a bark of relief that seemed to deflate his happiness, leaving a strained contentment behind.

"So now you're retiring."

"Now I'm retiring, after reaching an agreement with POTUS, the Committee and Congress on the fate of the BSI."

Color me intrigued. I understood why BB lied to me, it wasn't as if I hadn't told a few whoppers in my day when working for him, but the information overload sizzled across my skin and the vodka was definitely turning sour in my stomach. I gestured for him to continue, tell me how he wrangled with the Committee (comprised of four people: one from the Senate, a sitting Supreme Court judge, a member of the Joint Chiefs and a member of the President's cabinet, all theoretically capable of putting politics aside for the greater good) and the worst DC had to offer.

"Any potential Bureau Director has to be agreed upon unanimously by the Committee," BB explained, "from a pool of current Bureau employees. If they cannot agree on a candidate, then the next Director will be the most senior field agent."

"How in the wide, wide, world of sports did you manage that bit of magic?" I exclaimed. It was a feat not unlike achieving flight by flapping your hands *really* hard.

The smile came back full force and I knew what the next words out of his mouth would be. "I gave them you, Kal. I told them I was part of the old system, the old Bureau administration and what the government needed now was a face the people wanted to see, needed to see." A finger stabbed my way. "You. Someone the country can agree on ... mistrustful of authority, a loner, someone who can tell those in power to eff off and get away with it. All in all, it was the outcome I've been fighting toward so long and now it's here."

"But ... me?"

"You. I'm old school, and while you're considered ancient by Bureau standards—"

"Many thanks, Methuselah."

"Granted, I'm older than even you, but that's not the point. You're still youthful enough to piss into the wind and old enough to make the right decisions, assuming you don't go off the rails."

Fair point. My marbles weren't always in the same bag. "What if I say no?"

"Then the Committee will pick Davis."

Holy cats! Jefferson Woodrow Davis? The man who

thought the sun rose and set in his pants? The only thing worse than his ego was the bubonic plague.

BB's smile became grim. "Yes. Not my first or second or third pick, but he's a capable agent who looks good on paper and would make a competent Director."

Competent if you mean he'd put image before substance, but BB was right. Davis would keep the wheels greased ... and that's the problem. The Bureau needed more than just the status quo, it needed to grow, to change with the times and adapt to the future as it came barreling down the highway. The greasy, hot lump in my stomach bounced against my plummeting heart as I realized that I couldn't leave the Bureau in Davis' hands and even though I knew BB was manipulating me it was for the best of reasons, for the sake of the men and women of an institution he loved so dearly. I couldn't fault his logic or desire.

I would've done the same thing. Twice.

"Sure, I accept. One last op, though? For old time's sake?" My voice thickened slightly. I thought after another year I could turn my back on the Bureau, be shut of it and retire on my pension. For a sharp cookie, I tend to be more wrong than I'm comfortable with.

BB grinned even wider. I could see his molars. "Perfect. Just what I thought you'd say, and I have a doozy for you."

Fantastic.

CHAPTER TWO

Canton

Gardens of Bone

MY SPEAR FOUND A home in the guts of a quick-footed Trojan, sliding past the clamshell bronze breastplate, along the seam and through his left side. He spun, his heavy shield thudding into the haft of my spear, snapping it like a twig, but the movement was enough to swirl the head in his bowls and he let out a shriek of agony that fluted up, up, up until it gurgled away.

I dodged a short sword and spun, drawing my own as the other weapon whistled through the air where my neck was a moment ago. My arm lashed out and the tip of my sword licked over a shield to plunge beneath a chin, through a soft palate and into a brain, stopping only when the tip of the weapon struck the inside of my opponent's helmet.

"Well struck, cousin! How lucky am I to have a slayer such as yourself as part of my family?" Hard laughter shook the air, drowned out by screams, the clangor of weapons and the moans of the dying.

A shield rim flew toward my skull and I raised mine in time to avoid getting my brains well and truly scrambled. The two shields *clanged* and for a moment my arm went numb, so before the other warrior could take advantage, I swung and gave the guy a new red mouth to bleed from.

Beside me, the man who complemented my ability to slaughter others swung a blow so mighty that it cleaved through bronze shield, through the arm that held it and on down to split it completely in two. Before the shocked Trojan could even scream, the sword came back to thrust through an eye.

"Aah! Good fight!"

So, this was my cousin, the noble Diomedes, king of Argos. Big guy, flaming red hair and bloodthirsty as hell. In the two weeks since my arrival I found out his idea of sport was sex, fighting and fighting while having sex. Actually, that pretty much summed up the entire Greek army.

Another Trojan went for my knees with his spear, but I knocked it aside and leapt at him, thrusting my sword through his throat. Blood spouted from his mouth and he sagged. Another took his place.

The battle was nothing fancy, two armies charging at a rush, hitting with a resounding clash of shields and sprays of blood, shouts of anger, hatred and fear coupled with the terrifying shrieks of agony.

I'd been going at it for what seemed like a thousand years but was actually only a few minutes. As I tired, I fell back, and another eager Greek took my place at the shield line while I rested. The bitter, metallic taste of blood flooded my mouth and my shield arm felt sore and stringy, as if the tendons had been cut. I gulped big lungsful of air.

"This is the part I hate."

From my exhausted crouch I was face to crotch with the speaker, so I raised my eyes somewhat, so I could meet his eyes. It was Diomedes' good friend Odysseus, the great wanderer himself, although he hadn't yet reached the point that inspired Homer's *The Odyssey*.

"What?" I gasped in between breaths. The dude didn't even

look winded, although in his armor, he was sweating buckets in the summer sun. We all were. I bet we could fry eggs on our shields.

"I see your face, Cantoneades, and know how you feel about this war."

So much for Native American inscrutability. "That obvious?"

Odysseus shook his head, dyed-blue horsehair plume wobbling. "Only to those that share your distaste for bloodshed."

Well, color me purple call me a grape. I gaped, I goggled, my mind boggled. "You're one of the best I've ever seen!" I blurted.

"Being good at something," he replied, "doesn't mean you like it." With that out of the way, he shoved his way back into the war, pulling an exhausted warrior behind the lines and taking his place.

Mind still blown, I jumped back into the fray, throwing another tired warrior back to the reserves for a much needed break. The Greeks had a certain way of dealing with cowards ... not execution, no ... that would be a waste. They put them in the front lines during the first engagement, so they would have to fight or be turned into a gyro pretty doggone quick.

A shield slammed into mine and I thrust around, slicing at an exposed bicep. Blood spurted, and the Trojan cursed me in his strange, fluting accent, a liquid trill to the vowels. I made note ... some of that cussing was pretty original and I've been cussed at by the best. He retreated, his place being taken by another snarling Trojan.

Blood splattered my shield; my armor and my arms became lead weights attached to my shoulders as I hacked and slashed and thrust until my bronze short sword became so notched and blunted it was little better than a club.

Again, behind the lines among the reserves, panting and trying not to barf because I was so exhausted, exhausted from killing and being spattered with blood and brains and a bunch of other fluids I didn't want to think about and the ground beneath my sandals had turned to bloody mud that housed bits of shattered bone, torn flesh and splinters of teeth and it smelled awful, really worse than anything else I'd smelled before in my life and that's saying something considering that I was used to being hip deep in slavering undead on a regular basis.

"Cantoneades!"

What now? I rose from a crouch to peer above the helmets the front line. The fighting had stopped. At a whisker above six feet, I was practically a giant among the Greeks, whose diets and exercise regimen including fighting until bits fell off and eating anything that wasn't wriggling to get away. And a few things that were. Couple that with the lack of modern neonatal and childhood care and you had average height of about five-five, so I had a pretty good view of the person hollering for me.

Whoa. Big dude.

Not tall, just ... big, definitely the product of a good diet. About my height, but with enough muscle packed on for two professional wrestlers and their kids thrown in. Veins crawled like worms under bronzed skin beneath bronze armor so garishly crafted it was more a work of art than protection. His horsehair crest was colored a deep purple and flopped side to side with every motion of his head. A long, bushy beard flowed from his jaw to the middle of his sculpted breastplate and I felt a momentary touch of fear. He looked stronger than the Greek heavy hitter Ajax and meaner than that psychopath Achilles.

"Cantoneades!" He roared, looking around. The battlefield, our little section of the line, suddenly became still like the calm before a storm.

Uh-oh. This was bad. Bad like in imminent death kind of bad. Bad as in 'if things go like I think they're gonna go, my ass is toast' kind of bad.

The Greeks had this concept. It's called *arête*. Sort of means the highest quality in any sort of endeavor, or a kind of moral virtue. They were mad about it and single combat between heroes, such as Achilles and Hector in *The Iliad*, was the epitome of arête in their minds. When two heroes met in battle, it was the stuff of legends.

Thing is, I wasn't sure I qualified as hero material. Not that it mattered because when the big guy's brown eyes met mine, they practically blazed with glee. "There you are," he purred across the hushed crowd.

"Here I am," I agreed. "You know who I am, but do you mind giving me your name?"

He frowned. It was an expression to make children weep and I felt a large hand on my shoulder.

"What are you doing?" Diomedes hissed. "Don't you recognize him?"

I shook my head slightly keeping an eye on the Trojan's thunderous expression.

"That's Aeneas, the Dardanian ruler. Second only to Hector in combat and the equal to just about any other Greek." My cousin paused. "Including myself," he conceded. "He is a hero, so saying you don't know who the second most famous warrior in Troy is will bring repercussions."

Damn ... Aeneas. One of the only survivors of the fall of Troy and legendary warrior whose descendants founded Rome. In Virgil's *Aeneid* it was said that he could kill a bull with one punch of a cestus-covered fist. I shrugged off Diomedes' hand. I knew why Aeneas called for me. "What can he do? Kill me twice?" I stepped through the line, standing tall and keeping my eyes glued to his. "Sorry, noble Aeneas, but I was blinded by the blood of the Trojan heroes I've slain, I didn't get a good look at you." The whole crowd, Trojan and Greek, took in a deep breath in shock. Seemed like they weren't used to that kind of hero smack talk.

For a moment it looked like the big dude would chuck his spear my way, but then his mouth opened wide (really, these guys needed a good dental plan) and commenced to laughing his heroic ass off. He'd take a great big chest full of air, then spatter the field with laughter thick enough to spread on a cracker.

"You have a set of big, hairy balls, Greek," he bellowed between gales of mirth. "I heard tell of the new arrival from Argos crazy enough to drink lantern oil and piss on a fire! I love it!"

I was never going to understand these guys. "What do you want, Aeneas?"

The big warrior raised shield and spear. "You and me, single combat. Winner gets the loser's armor while the loser receives proper funeral rites."

Oh boy. My heart began to beat a hard tattoo in my chest and my stomach gave a slow roll. This was a capital 'H' Hero of legend and stuff, a guy who trained his whole life in armor, building up enough muscle to tear bricks apart with his bare hands. Me ... I was good with a gun, great with a knife and ...

Comes the dawn. "Agreed!" I said with a grin. Then I threw my shield to the ground.

The sounds of war faded, and silence reigned on the fields of Troy. Aeneas did the whole mouth wide open thing, along with a couple thousand other guys in their bronze underwear. From behind I heard a startled curse from Diomedes. I made a mental note about that one, something to do with a goat and a piece of cheese.

"Interesting," Odysseus said so softly to Diomedes I barely heard it.

"What?" Diomedes again.

"I think your cousin has a plan."

"For a funeral pyre, that's for sure!"

"I don't think so ..."

As for Aeneas, he took a few steps forward, lowering the long, leaf-shaped blade of his spear until it was pointed at the ground and away from my general direction. "What are you doing? Has Zeus struck you mad?"

I looked around. Yeah, the war had come to a complete halt and everyone was staring. Agamemnon (a complete douche and a half) stood in his chariot some fifty yards away, face clouded with confusion. Meanwhile the Trojans were starting to buzz. This was reality television at its best and bets were being laid on hot and heavy, but not in my favor I reckoned.

Grinning, I dropped my short sword into the bloody mud and shattered bits of bone, drawing another collective gasp as I stretched languidly, feeling every kink and knot of muscle unravel. Oh, that was good, I needed that, although I felt a large amount of discomfort at all the eyeballs looking my way. Still, it didn't stop me from stretching my body out, working out the sore and exhausted muscles that felt like wet taffy.

"What are you doing?" Aeneas repeated, goggling. You would've thought he'd never seen a Greek bend over and touch his toes while wearing armor before. He needed to get out more, that's for sure.

"Getting ready to beat you, Lord Aeneas." *Keep it calm, Canton, don't let him see how nervous you are.* "Give me a moment."

"What do you plan on fighting me with, then?"

It hit me then. The war ... it stopped. All the fighting, the bloody screams and the furious cries of enemies, the clang and clash of bronze against bronze, the creaking squeal of chariot wheels ... all gone. An eerie silence had descended upon the ruined Scamander plain, an air of pregnant expectancy flowing thick across everyone's skin like warm treacle. This was the stuff that birthed legends, that gave rise to stories that lasted a thousands of years, immortalized by poets, bards and dreamers.

I was smack in the middle of it. Damn.

I'd been thrust back in time into a story that formed one of the foundations of Western literature and somehow, by whatever agency, I'd been supplied an identity and backstory. Everything I needed to make my way in Ancient Greece, Asia Minor or wherever.

I had no idea how I got here. I knew who I was, where I worked, and I remembered every detail of my life ... except the events that led to me hobnobbing with bronze-clad macho men. *Temporal/special rifting due to quantum interference from his modern body.* Those words haunted me every waking moment, like a half-remembered song with that one lyric that drives you crazy for days on end.

Another thing that baked my noodle was the whole not being able to use modern idioms or words that didn't have a Greek equivalent. Sort of like an Interdiction that extended to concepts that wouldn't fit into this era. Really pissed me off, actually.

Enough doggone woolgathering, already. Time to get back to the present. Or the past. Or the past present future. Damn, this was going to give me headaches for years. Slowly, with as much showmanship I could muster, I drew a dagger, basically a long, thin triangle of bronze, unadorned and a little rough. It seemed these guys used daggers as a last resort, but for me, an Apache (a Greek Apache, it seemed), this was my jam.

I spun and flipped the dagger around, faster and faster, my fingers in total control of the razor-sharp weapon. Light glinted from the edges as I gave the Greeks and Trojan a real taste of what a true knife fighter could do. After a minute I flipped the dagger high, the blade practically humming as it spun so fast it appeared to be a bronze disk and caught it effortlessly by the hilt as it fell.

A collective "Oooohhhh!" from a thousand throats. I saw Diomedes suddenly grin behind his helmet. I guess I stood a chance against Aeneas after all. For a moment I worried about changing the timeline because killing Aeneas could mean that Rome would never be ... and that would be bad for Western civilization. Then again, Kal said time had a funny way of turning things to right so I had to rely on that. Rather weak tea as arguments went, but short of dying, what else could I do?

Once again Aeneas belched out some huge laughter and threw his own shield on the ground. Both the Trojans and the Greeks looked at him like he had a head full of rocks for giving up that kind of enormous advantage. "You must be hiding a bigger pair down there than your mad king Agamemnon, Cantoneades, I'll believe that, but let it not be said that Aeneas can't rise to a challenge. You have your pointy little dagger, and you're good with it, anyone can see that, but I am unbeaten with the cestus."

Oh boy. My heart nearly stopped.

With a flourish, he pulled from his belt a pair of thick gloves with knuckles padded in bronze plate. The leather looked old, well-worn and stained almost black with a combination of blood, sweat and other fluids I didn't want to think about. He slowly put them on and the Trojan warriors at his back began to chuckle while the Greeks started to look a bit concerned. Not that I could blame them, considering his reputation for killing oxen with a single blow while wearing those things. I knew that one good hit would powder the bones in my face and leave me with a serious dental bill.

"All right, Cantoneades. Have it your way." His grin showed more gaps than teeth.

Not to be outdone in the macho department, I began to shrug off my armor until I stood only in my leather war kilt, a token nod to modesty considering I wore nothing underneath. So, I stood there among the growing murmurs of alarm from my fellow Argives and the hoots and catcalls of the Trojans, cocking an eyebrow at my hulking opponent when he did exactly what I'd been hoping for.

He got naked. War kilt and all with nothing between him and the Olympus but atmosphere. There were more muscles under that skin than humans should be allowed to have. I swear I even saw his eyelids flex. He stood there, and he rippled, veiny and perfect. Scars crawled across his body like worms from tip to toes, but instead of taking away from the beauty of his form, they seemed right, a harmonious blend that amplified both his physical might and his air of impending violence.

The catcalls stopped. Once again silence descended until Aeneas said, "Nothing left to hide, no more excuses. Let's do this."

If his body was Adonis, then his face was Freddy Krueger. I tried to swallow in fear at the sight of his smashed nose and the thick ridges of scars across his cheeks and brow. This was a guy who'd been hit. A lot. Then hit some more until the hitter's arm got sore and he gave it up as a bad idea.

Every eye fell to me and I could feel the weight of them like Atlas' burden. My eyes searched the crowd, from the grinning Odysseus who gave me a broad wink, to the surly Agamemnon in his chariot to the clear space in which I stood, where nothing grew except yellowing bone. A giant garden of blood and death.

I hefted the dagger. "Yeah. Let's do this."

CHAPTER THREE

Kal

---·---

To The Rescue

JEANIE CAUGHT ME IN ARMORY as I was making a choice between lethal weaponry, both hidden and not. ARMORY had every bit of deadly nastiness that the Bureau could think of (that had been approved for use in the field, of course. After Canton's use of the Singularity spell in Chicago, further research into that bit of magical unpleasantness had been terminated. No one wanted a planet-sized hole where Earth used to be) and I was rarin' to equip myself for the next op.

"Kalevi Hakala, what are you doing?" Jeanie's English accent slid into my ears, soft, but with a hint of steel. She seemed a trifle unhappy. Okay, truthfully, she looked pissed. I guess I should've stopped by our quarters before haring off to ARMORY.

"Can't delay. Canton's in trouble." There, a Brave Bull P-38 SM. Fourteen in the clip, one in the pipe, just what the doctor ordered. That is if the doctor wanted to shred the Hippocratic oath and fill someone with lead. It would make a fine accompaniment to the Lahti, the Finnish 9mm that was a gift from dad.

Agent Tim Harker edged out the ARMORY door, not wanting to be anywhere near a lover's spat. They were building agents smarter and smarter these days. When he disappeared, Jeanie turned to me and her eyes went from winter frost to summer love in an instant. I breathed a sigh of relief. "Tell me," she said.

" 'Bout the time I went to St. Louis, the Bureau got a tip about that lady hitter from Omaha, you know, the one Canton called the Ninja Assassin Chick."

She nodded. The Omaha affair nearly punched her ticket. She about drained her body of all magic trying to save Canton from an explosive device and had Alex Dumont (our resident Super Genius) not been there to perform a magic transfusion, she would've died. My throat tightened just thinking about it. "And?"

"Well, Canton wanted her bad, went on a solo op with a full team shadowing to track her down. For some reason she'd been spotted by Ghost in Talladega, Alabama."

"The racing place?"

I shook my head. Ah, a monofilament garrote, one of the new ones that could cut through iron. Disguised as a Piaget wristwatch, it could be deployed in a manner of seconds. Very James Bond. "You're thinking the Superspeedway. I'm talking about the city, which is a few miles south. Anyway, Canton disappeared, along with the team. My guess is our Ninja Assassin Chick spotted him, which isn't so hard considering he's had about as much press as I have."

"Let me get this straight ... you, one of the most recognizable men in the United States, perhaps the world, plan on heading some secret op to find a woman who might have killed Canton and an entire Bureau team." Jeanie crossed her arms and a stubborn line appeared between her eyes. "Are you out of your bloody mind?"

"Granted, I should be tested, but that ain't gonna happen." Oh, look, punch knives disguised as a belt buckle. I loved those. "This is my last op, this is Canton we're talking about.

If he's alive." *Please, no ifs*. My mind shied away from the possibility that he was no longer in my life. "I aim to find him and bring him back."

"So, BB is finally retiring and leaving you with the job."

What? "What?"

Jeanie rolled her beautiful eyes. "You are so damn clueless. It's been the worst kept secret in the Bureau. Everyone knew BB was retiring and planning on having you succeed him as Director." I wasn't looking at her, but I could hear her eyes rolling. "Honestly, if you weren't so bloody smart I'd think you were a moron."

Ah, there ... the new Jamieson Belt Sword. Nice little gadget. Looked and felt like an ordinary dress belt but twist the buckle (which had been modified to hold two punch knives) and the semi-fluid inner core became a rapier while the leather acted as a sheath. Not much of a hilt, but a definite surprise for the bad guys. Is that a sword around your waist or you happy to see me? "I can't think about that right now. Can't think about anything but this op. I'm going to be shadowed by teams Beta and Gamma and I'll have my own personal satellite tasked to my location at all times. If I fart, the teams will know what it smells like, so I'm as safe as I'm ever going to get."

Warm hands cupped my face. "You dear, sweet idiot. What makes you think your handsome face won't be recognized?"

Ah, will you look at that! A ball point pen with the explosive power of a pound of C4. Gotta have me some. I tucked it into my shirt pocket. "That's where you come in, dear. BB said you've been working on long-term disguise spells."

Forcing my head so I'd have to look her dead in her eyes, Jeanie said, "Yes, I can help you, but you have to realize this op sounds crazy. Crazy bad."

"I get it, hon, but this is something I have to do." Canton was alive. He had to be, there were no other options. There, a pair of Ecco shoes, the perfect accompaniment to my ensemble.

"Understood, but I'm going to be part of the team that shadows you."

Oh *hell* no. Before I could say anything, she placed a hand over my mouth, sealing my lips as effectively as if they were welded shut. Yeah, she always had that effect on me.

"You certainly weren't about to object, were you?"

Okay, *you* try arguing with a smart, capable, intelligent woman who just so happens to be your wife, and a magician. Utterly frightening when she puts her mind to it. All I could do was gently shake my head.

"Good. When you're done here, join me in Special Branch." With that she was gone, leaving only a faint trace of Chanel and natural musk that never failed to rev my engines.

Back to stuffing my pockets with all sorts of lethal goodies. This was better than Christmas.

***

LATER ON, IN SPECIAL BRANCH, I sat on a stool feeling like a naughty schoolkid while Jeanie and Alex looked me over like a prize pig at the county fair. Where was Charlotte the spider when I needed her? Would her web read 'Some Agent'?

"What are you thinking, Jeanie? A Distraction Spell?" Alex eyed me critically with all four eyes.

Let me tell you about our resident Wunderkind … he had more brains than any twelve Rhode Scholars with a couple of Nobel Laureates thrown in for spice. Most might be fooled by the birth control glasses or his unfortunate preference for sweater vests (really, the kid was a walking billboard for bad taste), but he went through a slightly shortened version of agent training at Coronado and could probably smash through a barroom full of disgruntled bikers. Not to mention that he was one of the world's foremost wizards and could turn your brains into mint jelly. All that mental acuity was currently focused on yours truly with laser-like precision. It kind of creeped me out, but I wasn't about to tell him that.

"You're creeping him out, Alex." Jeanie gently steered the genius away, shooing him off toward the gaggle of technogeeknerds that were trying not to stare. Said techno-geeknerds comprised the rest of the Special Branch R&D staff currently on duty, a serious nerd festival that rivaled anything ever seen at a Star Trek convention. "Besides," she continued, staring deep into my eyes, "too many things to go wrong. I think a few slight modifications such as hair, skin tone, nose and jawline and no one will recognize him." She tapped a long fingernail against my forehead. "Maybe make him a little ugly."

"Can't happen, beautiful, you can't ugly this mug up … it'd be a sin."

That earned me a rather loud eyeroll. Alex sniggered behind his hand.

"Then let's go for different," Jeanie mused. She laid her palms on either side of my face and for an instant her deep brown eyes that never failed to capture me flashed an actinic blue. There came a tingle that skittered all over the skin of my face like an electric mouse. I wanted to sneeze. I wanted to scream in disgust, but I was pretty sure I'd lose some man-points on that one.

"No, no, no …" Alex waved his hands. "We need more."

I stared. "More? My face just feels like a rodent with twenty-thousand volts shot up its ass ran all over it and you think I need more?"

Before I could blink, Alex was on me like glitter on a strip-per, hands cupping my chin and eyes boring into mine, holding me fast, pinning me to the stool. Wormy heat slithered over my skull, around my left eye and across my lower face. My skin twitched, then twitched some more as goosepimples raced to and fro and that static tingle came back, but instead of an elec-tric mouse, it felt like the lower half of my face was trying to take a shot for freedom and crawl away at flank speed.

I couldn't scream, couldn't yell, couldn't even bat an eye, but I sure wanted to. I wanted to slap my cheeks until they bled, holler at my wife to make the bad feelings go away be-cause they kept building and building until my vision swam from unshed tears and I couldn't even wipe my eyes, my muscles were not my own.

Back in the day, my rage, the magical enhancement to my strength and speed, would've countered Alex's spell, but that was long gone now (it's a story for a quiet night and far too much vodka), so I had to suffer like a regular Straight.

Sucks being on the crap end of the stick.

As abruptly as it began, it was gone, and I had my muscles back. There must've been a murderous glare on my face because Alex and the rest of the technogeeknerds took a collective step back. Pretty sure I was an inch away from foaming at the mouth.

"What the bloody hell did you do to me, kid?" I snarled.

"Now now, Kal, had to be done. You look great! Doesn't he look great everyone?" He turned to the gaggle (herd, murder, flock) of Special Branch types.

"Yeah, great!" Enthusiastic nods all around while one cute little scientist said, "He looks hot."

That got Jeanie's attention. She tossed the hapless cutie a snarly look that could've curdled cream and fetched a mirror. "Here."

There I was! Except, there I wasn't. My skull hadn't changed shape or anything, but the face that fronted it was that of a stranger. Slightly olive skin, a short, dark brown beard, a nose that most would consider Roman, brown eyes and a tangle of curly brown hair the color of heavily tanned leather, just a couple shades short of black. But that wasn't the kicker by a long shot because my two trusted magicians, one the love of my life, the other the most annoying brainiac I'd ever met, decided that the whole ensemble wouldn't jibe without scars. Two of them. One above my left eye about an inch-long running vertically bisecting my eyebrow. The next one started below the left eye and ran for another inch to the middle of the cheek. It looked like someone tried to slice me in two but missed. Barely.

"Scarred." What the hell? I had enough scars, thank you very much! "You scarred me! You colossal dick!"

A babble of voice erupted as I vaulted off the stool. Jeanie put herself between me and a soon-to-be-human-pretzel little geek magician. "Now, now, love, let's not be hasty."

Hasty? Hasty? Words wouldn't come, all I could do was my landed fish impression.

"You look great, love."

"Yeah, great!" "Totes hot, Kal." "Sincerely, dude." And more along these lines. It wasn't that I was upset about having scars, it was the fact that I didn't earn them honestly by killing a Supernatural or three. Still, my jets began to cool a bit and I found my seat while giving the little skink Alex the old evil eye. *Revenge is a dish best served with your gonads on a platter, kid.* That thought comforted me.

"Uh, Jeanie?" This from the cute technogeeknerd who still had her eyeballs plastered to my face. "He still sounds like Kal. Can we do something with his voice?"

Okay, no Christmas gift for her.

My wife tapped her front tooth with a short fingernail as she considered me carefully. A little worm of unease turned in my gut.

"Yes," she said. "You're right, Thelma. We need to address this."

Thelma? My wife was taking advice from a Thelma? I wanted to scream and shout, but Jeanie was giving me the old bug eyes, pinning me to the stool. Swirling away, she headed toward a set of metal drawers against the near wall and rifled through the contents. After a moment she came back carrying a silver herringbone bracelet. "Here."

"Awww, and I didn't get you anything."

"Don't be a smarty-pants. Put it on."

Hey, I wore the pants in this relationship, I wasn't about to take orders. However, I certainly knew when my choices were limited, so I snapped it in place on my left wrist. I gave it a shake, gave it a wiggle, but I didn't even feel a tingle. No scratches in the bumper or anything. That worried more than high-voltage rodents.

"Perfect," Jeanie murmured and placed her hands around my wrist, covering the bracelet. A flash of her eyes later and she removed her hands. The bracelet was gone.

"What happened? Nothing happened, did it?"

Nothing was all I got … that and a whole bunch of staring. Eyeballs as far as I could see.

"What? You're bloody making me nervous, you lot are."

And there it was, the sound of the penny dropping. Of a whole bank full of pennies dropping. On my head. Over and over. I put my head in my hands.

"British … you've given me a British accent, haven't you? Blimey, I sound like I should be watching footies cheering on Manchester United."

Laughter. Lots of laughter. Fantastic.

"Actually, love, you'd root for Liverpool." It looked suspiciously as if the love of my life's face contorted like a rubber Halloween mask in a failed attempt to tamp down on a belly laugh. Surely not.

"Wonderful. You couldn't make it sound like someone who'd cheer for a real football team, could you?" My voice sounded huskier, hoarser than normal with a hard, metallic edge.

More laughter. I thought Alex might birth some kittens, while the cute technogeeknerd who thought I looked hot alternated between outright lust and mirth. Glad to be such an emotional inspiration.

"And my speech patterns? What, how did you do that I'm wondering?" My nerves, already frayed by the physical change, unraveled some more as I realized I sounded like a *Downton Abbey* character.

"All part of the package," Jeanie replied, taking the sting out of the situation with a kiss. Maybe I could forgive her. "The bracelet is now part of your body, inside you so it can't be removed, but its magic can be heard."

A bracelet *inside* my body? Okay, this was worse than facing a herd of Ogres or ghouls. A bracelet inside my body working its magic was just … just … *gross*.

"I'm going to be sore about this for a while, aren't I?"

She slipped her arms around my neck and the other people went away for a while.

Okay, I forgave her.

CHAPTER FOUR

Canton

———•———

Blood Sport

IN THE AIR BEFORE Aeneas could ready himself, dagger darting for a soft spot. He moved pretty damn quick for a such a doggone big man and I only managed to raise a thin slice of blood along his forearm.

I slid across the bloody mud, feeling a piece of bone tear a furrow along my thigh, but I was too busy to feel pain because the Incredible Trojan Hulk was trying to mash my brains out through the back of my head.

A fist the size of a country ham slammed into the mud where my head had been the moment before. It sank in a good six inches and Aeneas gave a grunt of frustration as I rolled away and quickly stood.

"You're fast," he grunted, flinging the muck from his cestus. "But I'm not slow, either." The grin of pure, lustful, violent glee on his face sent an icicle down my spine.

No time for fear, though, as I darted in, ducking a haymaker that would've put my jaw somewhere in Egypt and went for a gut shot, but a bronze and leather clad hand slapped the dagger away and shoved me hard enough that I landed on the flat of my ass.

A big foot tried to mash my testicles into the mud, but I scissored away, adrenalin providing me with just enough *oomph* to dodge. I made it to my feet in time to catch a foot in the hip. A white-hot splinter of pain raced up my side and I pushed away with the one leg that didn't go numb in an instant and the crowd of warriors roared, the Trojans in glee and the Greeks in despair. I would've roared too, but I was trying not to scream instead because as I backed away the pain from my hip shattered any coherent thought.

Not broken, but hurt, the muscle and bone deeply bruised and aching with every stumbling step. The kind of hurt that would slow me down some, perhaps enough for that monstrous Trojan to knock my block off. *Doggone it … I could actually lose.*

Aeneas tried for an uppercut, which might have connected if I wasn't expecting it, but I managed to stumble to the right. The fist whistled past my cheek and I slashed it in a clean miss to keep the big guy at bay.

A lunge, hoping to catch him off guard, but my hip took that moment to refuse service (logical considering I wasn't wearing a shirt or shoes) and I stumbled in time to catch a bronzed fist to the side.

Ever have a moment of sheer, mind-numbing pain? The kick-in-the-crotch, finger-cut-off, lung-seizing moment that turns all the lights off for a hot second where even time becomes a spectator to the horrible events that conspire against you?

That big fist wrapped in bronze and leather hit with the force of a runaway train and I felt ribs give with a sickening crunch and everything was gone, gone, gone as my breath went to far away places and my will to live decided it was time for a coffee break.

I managed not to fall on my face as I fought for breath, the roar of Trojan bloodlust as well as the wail of anguished

Greeks thudding into my ears, but I did dodge the next blow. Somewhat. A left jab that slid across my cheek, tearing the skin open under my eye in a quick, ripping rush of pain.

More groans and I could see some of my fellow warriors tearing at their hair. Dang, but these Greeks were an emotional bunch.

Another jab, but I brushed it aside almost automatically as I tried to breathe, tried to do anything, tried not to die messily. Black spots danced in front of my eyes and, as I ducked another jab, my diaphragm finally unclenched its grip on my lungs.

Air!

Ouch.

Ribs hollered. They screamed and threw a major fit as I felt them grind in my chest and every breath was fire, every movement ground glass against frayed nerves and I wanted to cry, wanted to scream, but I didn't have the breath, not enough to fill out a good yell. All I had was the growing panic and the morbid certainty that I was about to die, flattened to a pulp by a man three thousand years dead in my time.

I staggered away from the next punch and the next, and the one after that, each dodge a little slower because of the fire in my ribs, the broken glass feeling of shattered bone. He was fast, faster than my buddy Kal, faster than a guy that big had any right to be. Stabbing him meant getting close to those fists and the sheer carnage they were capable of dishing out, and that thought frightened me.

Wait. What? Frightened? Me?

Since I couldn't speak in modern idioms or slang and couldn't even *try* to speak of those things that wasn't already known in the Bronze Age of the Greek culture, it didn't mean I couldn't *think* them. I still had all my twenty-first century knowledge, my twenty-first century training and I let fear and the Trojan's awesome reputation cloud my thinking.

Looks like I brought the wrong weapon to this fight.

As Kal would say, 'I may be slow, but I get there.' If I couldn't talk or write (wasn't even sure I was literate in this day and age), I could sure as hell *do* something about it.

I was trying to fight old school. Time for new school. Krav Maga wouldn't be invented for a few millennia, but that wasn't going to stop me from using it, but it was going to hurt awful.

The dagger fell from my hand as if I lacked the strength to hold and my opponent pasted a grin on his shattered and scarred features, a man realizing he was about to finish the fight in his favor.

A punch came my way, a haymaker and I stepped in, blocking with my left arm and boy did my doggone side hate that. I could almost hear a ripping, tearing sound coming from deep within my torso as fire shot to my skull and at the same time my left forearm went numb blocking Aeneas' arm, my right fist shot forward striking the big guy under the chin. His head snapped back, and I took another step, hooking my right heel behind his and I pushed.

Down went the jolly Trojan giant, splat into the rusty mud, me riding him down all the way, my knee against his chest and when he hit, my knee did some dirty to his sternum. I think I heard a pop, if not a snap and a crackle.

Then it was time for my fist work.

Fists to throat and nose, a thumb to the eye and a right hook that I folded in, so I struck his ruined nose with my elbow rather than fist. It burst like a rotten tomato and I tasted blood on my teeth. Again and again, punching, punching, punching, while one of the greatest heroes in history lay there and took it, gagging from the jab to the throat, choking on the blood from his nose and I didn't even feel my side, there was no pain, only the elation of victory, of defeating an enemy that was fixing to turn me into sauce.

Done. Aeneas lay there, semi-conscious, barely breathing and I arched my back, thrust my head to the sky and whooped it up, giving voice to the victory cry of my ancestors. Tarzan eat your heart out.

Two words broke the sudden silence. "Kill him!" That

from Agamemnon in his chariot. Asswipe. I didn't bother to acknowledge the king of the Greeks, instead I stood up, each rising inch shredding agony as my ribs protested through the fading adrenalin rush.

No one spoke. All around three thousand hardened warriors stared at me, most with slack mouths, catching the carrion flies that were the mainstay of any bloody battlefield.

My vision swam, the world tilted one way and then the next. Diomedes stood with Odysseus, staring as I took first one step, then another. More tilting, my head felt full of rotten cotton and my ribs were a hot mess that stole each breath my lungs tried to take. Heat ate at my skin and my torn cheek cribbled blood down to my chin and onto my chest. Compared to my ribs, rent flesh on my face was doggone weak as circus lemonade.

"Cantoneades, cousin." Diomedes' words trailed off as he caught me right before I passed out.

***

"WHY DIDN'T YOU JUST KILL him?" raged the King.

One thing about Agamemnon, he used to be a great man. Not tall, not wide, but solid like a chunk of iron with a beautiful head of hair so black it seemed to absorb light and so long it fanned around his body to his waist. In war he put all that hair up in a que and lashed it close to his skull so no enemy could have a convenient handle to grasp. His muscles moved like oiled snakes beneath his dark, sun-kissed skin, but there was a goodly layer of lard there, too, giving him a pot belly approaching a pony keg in size, barely hidden by the white and burgundy length of cloth that covered his body called a *himation*.

He *used* to be great, but time, greed and obsession changed him from a warrior king to a dissipated despot whose only concern was fulfilling his every whim, slaking his thirst for conquest. Drink exploded the capillaries across his nose and yellowed his eyes while frustration added more lines to his face than age could account for.

"A Trojan hero, *the* Trojan hero next to Hector, could have been removed from combat. Your merciful actions have doomed several of your brother warriors, you addle minded whoreson!"

All I could do was lie there and take it, eat his crap and wait for him to finish. My tent was large enough to house Odysseus, Diomedes (who didn't seem to be too pleased as his boss chewed me out), Agamemnon, my slave—doggone it, the *girl,* no matter how well put together she was—and me. Also, calling her a slave, having a slave, made me sick to my stomach. I'd long since vowed to free her once we got out of this mess. While freeing her now would be fine and dandy, having the other Greeks see her as my property afforded her a measure of safety. Perhaps it was a degree of how much this new old world was affecting me that it took a week for me realize I never asked for her name. Talya.

That tent was sure crowded, though. Crowded enough that when Agamemnon shouted I could tell that his mouthwash wasn't cutting it.

"It was his battle," Odysseus said, arms crossed. While Diomedes wore a red himation and Agamemnon's was white and burgundy, the small king simply wore a wrap around his loins called a breechclout. As a guy who practically lived at sea, it showed in a strong streak of pragmatism. "It was his choice to grant mercy." He had a great, big brain packed into a little body. Shorter than most Greeks, hovering around five-foot flat, he made up for his diminutive size with enough muscle to put a gymnast to shame. I would've thought that kind of muscle would slow him up some and ruin his flexibility but watching him wield a spear put paid to that idea and then some. There was no one in the Greek army who could match him with a spear. Of course, Achilles, that young psychopath, was fast enough to carve him up if they both used short swords, but a spear? No way in hell. I guess what Odysseus lacked in height, he made up with that six-foot polearm.

Agamemnon fumed. He steamed. He turned a bright shade of puce. It was actually kinda fun to watch and I did so with growing amusement tempered by the aching pain under the stitches on my cheek. When they came out I'd have a hell of a scar. Probably all purple-y and gross considering the medical technology of the time. I'm just glad Talya boiled the stitches like I commanded before sewing my face shut. Boy, that *hurt*. Every draw of the gut string felt like termites burrowing in my skin, tearing through nerve, fat and muscle. At least I didn't scream.

The jerk who would be emperor muttered curses so vile that I think even Kal would've taken notes while Odysseus continued to stare a hole in him. Agamemnon wasn't scared of anybody, his army was too powerful, his legend still too bright for anyone to challenge him, but the small king of the tiny island of Ithaca unnerved him in some manner I'd yet to divine. Maybe Agamemnon was afraid that Odysseus was smart enough to get away with murder.

Finally, my cousin Diomedes (still didn't know how I arrived here with a complete backstory) said, "Cantoneades has claimed his prize in Aeneas' armor and forged a legend with his unusual wrestling skills. Let him have the tent, he needs to rest and heal. Those ribs will take time to become whole." With that he ushered the other kings out.

Time to heal was right. My ribs were a broken mess and the battle was called off for the day, so the warriors could sit around the fires and tell the story of Cantoneades versus the great Aeneas. Without television or the Internet to numb their minds, ancient peoples told stories and held sporting competitions to entertain themselves and this particular tale looked to be on its way to be a doozy. So, with the Trojans back behind their walls performing funeral rights for the fallen and the Greeks behind the palisade telling tales and performing funeral rights for their fallen, I had some time to lie back and marvel at the ginormous purple-black bruise covering the left side of my torso.

Talya offered me a cup of wine, which I took gratefully even though it tasted like fermented cat's piss. Drinking regular water would've had me headed straight for a little town called Dysentaryville, right next to Vomitania and across the bay to Diarrheaberg. There were more little critters in the water here than Sea World.

Blech. The wine had definitely turned, but vinegar was better than squatting over a pot for a week, so I downed it all while my bound ribs told me what a fool I'd been. Talya snuggled down against me, careful of my side, and gently kissed my neck.

"I am glad you survived a killer such as the great Aeneas, my lord," she murmured, nuzzling.

Only a girl. You have socks older than her, you perv! I understood that kids grew up early in ancient times, but doggone it, I still had modern sensibilities. My body, despite the damage, wanted to get busy with her, but my mind gave my libido the finger and the mind is the master of the body. Normally.

This was no normal situation. Not by a long stretch.

"Is my lord well?" Talya inquired.

For two weeks I barely touched her except to gently push her away, giving the excuse that I was fatigued, or that I needed to concentrate on the next battle, although she made it clear that there were ways to ease any tension I may have.

Not too terribly long ago fellow agent and love of my life, Winch, died horribly at the hands (or more precisely, jaws) of a Supernatural near San Francisco and the loss hit me worse than I ever thought possible. A great gaping emptiness that threatened to tear my soul out through my nose.

Doggone it, I missed her every day. My throat tried to close up and I swallowed reflexively, coughing slightly and wincing as my ribs pinched hard.

Talya must have caught sight of my expression. "My lord?"

"Memories, Talya. Just memories."

She nodded. "Tell me, my lord, that I may share their burden."

I shook my head and the straw pillow underneath rustled. My eyes tried to water.

The furs slid and shimmied as Talya snuggled closer and it was then I realized she shrugged out of her short little shift called an *exomis*. There was nothing between her skin and mine except a few molecules of air.

Just a girl and far too young for the likes of you. I tried to imagine what my grandfather, Nantan Lupan, would say, but Talya's hands roamed all over my tummy and I could see his lips move, but the words were lost with the rasp of her nails across my skin.

"My lord, you are tense, so please share with me what is on your mind."

No doggone way.

"Please, my lord, open up to me." Soft palms stroked my good cheek. The stiches on my wound felt hot and tight. "Relax, open your mind to me so that I may share your discomfort, share your discontent that you may not be so burdened. Know that I am with you now and forever, free or slave, I will never leave your house, so you know that when you open up to me we will share a burden that will never leave this tent, for what is between us is only between us, shared and held close, a burden lightened by love and desire."

Love and desire … yes.

"For when we share, we are made free, when we surrender to others, then we gain strength in numbers. Surrender your burdens to me, my lord, and be free, find it in your loving heart to open your mind to me."

Yes. Open up. Talya's words comforted, soothed because they were true. Sharing healed. My eyelids grew heavy.

"Be with me, my lord, because I need you. Share with me

because you need me. Together we are strong, we can survive the Plains of Ilium, we can survive *anything*. We can do this, but only if you open up to me."

Languid and languorous, warm ... so warm and content, the feel of her body next to mine and the slow drifting on to that place between sleep and awake where the spirits of my ancestors could reach out and whisper in my ear. *Nantan Lupan, grandfather, are you there?*

I am here grandson ...

"Open up to me, Cantoneades, let me in ... "

Please, Nantan Lupan, help me. What should I do?

"Open, my brave warrior."

My soaring hawk, Itza-Chu, listen to the woman. She seems pretty smart.

"Let me in."

So tired, grandfather.

"That's it ..."

You have no Interdiction here, grandson, nothing to keep your mind closed and lonely.

"Ahhh ..."

Wait. What?

A cold shiver hit me like a sledgehammer made of ice and I bolted upright, the furs flying and my side screaming. Talya cursed and hopped away, fear scrawled on her face.

"This is wrong," I said. "Bad wrong."

"My lord?"

Before I could respond, the far wall of the tent shimmered and swirled around a point some three feet in the air, spinning as a circle of darkness opened up and swallowed me whole. As my mind stretched like a rubber band on the verge of snapping, I heard Talya scream in anger.

CHAPTER FIVE

Kal

———•———

On The Hunt

THE FIRST STEP WAS landing in Birmingham where I rented a new-ish Ford Fusion and headed east toward Talladega on the 20 until I hit 77 south to the city. Most people think NASCAR when they think Talladega, but it was the city that swallowed Canton whole, so that's where I needed to be.

All agents had nanolocators, pinhead sized tracking devices implanted into a butt cheek and they allowed location of an agent at any given time. Canton's locater went offline a few days ago shortly before I finished the St. Louis op and that's what raised a kerfuffle with BB.

"Only six point three miles until you reach Talladega, Agent Hakala," Spooky droned through my smartphone. No bone-induction patch for a bloke undercover.

Ugh … Spooky. Used to be the Bureau had its own cyber specter called Ghost, a MIT kid who, with the untrained help of a much younger brainiac Alex, translated himself into a computer and from there the Internet. Immensely powerful, patriotic and ethical, he was the Bureau's secret weapon against the Supernatural world.

During the St. Louis op, however, I managed to grant Ghost's fondest wish, to become human again. Thanks to a major D-bag of a demon (actually, they're all D-bags, but the demon Ornias took the taco on douchebaggery), I came into the possession of male body in tip top shape. The mind was a lost cause, but there was brain enough to re-house an intellect, so I enlisted Alex and we manhandled Ghost's essence into the body of that brain-dead man.

Right now, the man formerly known as Ghost was learning how to deal with flesh and blood after years of doing without. I hear he should be out of adult diapers soon.

Before he turned from cyber to corporeal, he created an AI program called Spooky, a program with so many restrictions upon self-replicating and self-altering, lacking even the barest hint of ambition or drive that it lay in BB's computer like a lump just thinking strange electronic thoughts until summoned. Sure, it was efficient and reliable, but it had the personality of a potato. Creeped me clean the hell out.

"I understand, Spooky, really I do. Kind of you, but really no need to remind me when I'm this close, is there?"

"No sir."

"And please don't call me Agent Hakala over the mobile considering I'm undercover. Keep it to Mr. Murray."

"I will comply."

Of course, you will, you wank. Lord, I missed Ghost. Glad he was human again, but in his cyber existence you knew that when you talked to him there was something there that understood, could empathize.

From the 77 into Talladega I turned a slight right onto East St., following the prompts from the smart phone toward my destination. The architecture was a mixture of modern and turn of the century quaint that usually houses mom-and-pop stores and unique boutiques along with the occasional Mexican restaurant thrown in for something different. The place I wanted to find was a bar/restaurant called Nina's, the type of place commonly referred to as a gastropub.

It was the only place Canton visited before disappearing and first of three places the team visited in an attempt to locate him before they, too, disappeared. My money was on nefarious deeds a-brewing in Nina's and I was aiming to uncover them ... then cause some serious mayhem.

Heat and humidity slapped my face as my shoes hit the sidewalk and I hurried into the pub, so I wouldn't sweat the important bits of my body off and found that the A/C had been cranked to such a low temperature that I thought icicles were forming on my eyebrows.

Unlike most bars, Nina's let in a lot of light, large windows opening up onto Battle St. and giving it an airy feeling of comfort. Small booths lined one wall and I sat at the first one I could, the place not yet reaching the height of the lunch rush. I checked my watch. Eleven oh five. I made good time.

A whole lotta waitress swayed over to the booth, her big self tucked in tight into a black number that barely reached her knees. A menu smacked the table in front of me. It was indecently thick. "Hiya, handsome," she said with a bat of false eyelashes. "What can I do for you?"

Lose fifty pounds of makeup and get a new dress. Unkind thought, that. I was too on-edge, too angry about my best friend now missing. *He's not dead. He's not.* "Well, love, I'm feeling peckish I am. What do you recommend?"

"Ooooo," she cooed. "English fella. We don't get many of those around these parts. For you, hon, I recommend the tri-tip open faced sandwich with garlic and cheddar mashed potatoes. They're real good."

"Sounds good to me, love." I heaved and managed to deposit the menu back into her arms. "And a spot of tea would be grand."

"Iced or hot, hon?"

"Hot of course, with a spot of milk and cream, dear."

She winked. "Yes indeed." That said she staggered off under her menu load to deliver my order.

What did Canton order here? Who did he talk to? His daily

briefs were adequately named; BB knew only that he posed as a Federal Marshall looking for a woman to deliver a warrant. His car, now towed, had been parked outside the restaurant, but no hide or hair of the Apache to be found. Normally the FBI would be all over Talladega like east coast jackrabbits trying to locate my friend, but BB wanted this handled in-house and thought I would have more luck.

Sure, hoped he was right.

As for the ninja assassin chick, it was Ghost who found her, oddly enough. Thanks to the best in magic and tech, the Bureau possessed an accurate likeness, accurate enough that she was spotted by traffic cam on the corner of Battle and Court streets and alerted BB, who gave the op to Canton seeing how he fought her once before and came out on top during the op in Omaha.

The tea came along with another wink and a sashay that allowed me to see exactly how proud the waitress was of the junk in her trunk.

"How long have you worked here?" I asked the waitress when she came back with my food. Smelled wonderful … big juicy pieces of tri-tip in brown gravy that had just the barest hint of cinnamon and the garlic mash had just the right number of lumps to seem home-made, yet smooth and creamy enough to show true artistry in the cooking.

"Oh, about eight years now, hon," said the waitress, bending over slightly. I noticed (couldn't help it … far too obvious) that the top button of her black blouse had come undone. Her … attributes were displayed quite nicely. "Every day except Sunday. That's the Lord's day, you know."

Beware, here be dragons.

Back to the issue at hand. Between big meaty bites, I pulled out my cell and fetched up a pic of Canton and showed it to her. "Have you seen this man, my dear? He's gone missing and I'm looking to find him, I am."

Fifteen feet behind the waitress I saw the bartender, a well-built bloke with two full sleeves of tats, frown thunderously as he caught my words. As for my server, her face screwed up tighter than a miser's purse and she quickly shook her head and trundled off as fast as her bulk allowed.

Fantastic. A clean hit. These folks definitely knew something if that bartender's face meant anything, and it did. For a moment I felt the trill of the hunt, the bold opening of a chess game that would involve guns and blood and death. I could've been subtler, but where's the fun in that?

The waitress didn't come back. The person who did come to see me was the big bartender with the sleeve tats and the face all closed up and sour. "I'm afraid I'm going to ask you to leave, mister. Don't worry about paying, the chow is on the house." He loomed.

Really, it was a good loom. I'd been loomed at by the best. He wanted me to object so he could ripple his muscles and commence to doing me some harm. The desire to break me like balsa wood was writ large on his barred face. Boy, did I ever want for him to give it a try.

Maybe I was growing up, maturing. Nope, that's not it. The truth was I didn't need that kind of distraction. I had an Apache to find and this hyper-muscled douchebag wasn't going to get in my way and ruin the party.

Plan B. My Marshall's badge hit the table with a solid *thunk*. Man, they made those things solid.

Mister Bartender's face went from shut to fear in about two seconds. It didn't help him any that my left hand had drifted out of sight as if my fingers were caressing the butt of a, oh say, a Finnish Lahti L-35. Often mistaken for a German P38, the 9mm pistol was heavy, reliable and, in the right hand, could shoot the eyebrows off a politician from a hundred feet.

Damn right he should've been scared. "Listen, mate, I am a duly sworn Deputy Marshall of these United States here on official business. If you intend on being such a bloody fool, at least wait until I have finished eating me meal." For some reason the newly added scar over my eye throbbed a bit.

The big guy chose the better part of valor, which was

scuttling away with his tail between his legs and I went back to consuming my particularly tasty meal. I made note to get the recipe for the mash. Top notch, really.

I tossed a couple of quid … ah … dollars onto the table for the waitress and headed out. Time for the second place Canton's shadow team visited before disappearing.

Rumble Joe's Gym. Looked like it sounded, a brick-faced two-story just down the street less than a block-and-a-half away, where musclebound types pumped serious iron and took their fists to the heavy bag. I decided to hoof it since it was so close and as I let the heat of the day wash over me I wondered what brought the team to such a seedy looking joint. Were they being thorough, or did a witness come forward with some information?

Perhaps the A/C had a heart attack and decided to take a decade or two off because the humidity outside was outpaced by the thick air inside. The stale fried chicken odor of hard sweating assaulted my nose and the sounds of weights clanking against each other filled the air. Next to the door lay the reception desk, a worn little podium where an even more worn looking old man sat reading the paper through a set of half-moon glasses chained around his neck.

"Yeah?" he droned as I drew near.

"Can I see the owner, mate?"

Washed out blues flicked my way then back to the paper. "Not in."

"Mind calling him?"

"Yeah, I do." Still reading the paper. What was so fascinating?

Two portraits of Benjamin Franklin glided onto the podium along with the cell with a pic of Dover Harkness, the team leader. "How about this gent then, sport? You've seen him around, have you?"

Lo and behold the little old dude must've been part leprechaun because he made those C-notes disappear faster than a politician's promise. One second there, then *bam!* … not.

"Little over a week ago," said the amateur magician. "This

hard case comes in and like you shows a picture of a cute gal saying he has to serve a warrant. Also showed me a picture of some Indian-looking fella. The hard case carried a Marshal's badge and everything." Blue the color of the sky near the desert sun peered at me over reading glasses. "You ain't no fed, though. No fed deals greenbacks, they just threaten. Besides, ain't no British feds here."

What he said jibed with the timeline. "You never know, mate, I may surprise you, mightn't I?"

"Doubt it."

Okay. Good enough for now, I could always come back later. Time for the third place on the list.

Back on the sidewalk, but not alone. Five guys, all fit, all grim, dressed in leather vests, T-shirts, and rather dodgy blue jeans. Most had tats, the man in front tatted up the most.

Without a word the man in front nodded toward the open door of a black cargo van that practically screamed 'vehicle used for nefarious purposes, stay back 200 feet' and the little Capt. Kirk in my brain kicked my mind into warp twelve as I assessed the situation in a matter of seconds.

The tats. Fake, had to be, too gloriously colored to be real. Henna and such at a guess. That meant the tough guy outfits were for intimidation, as were the various earrings, nose rings and gauges, all window dressing. Pros, all of them by the way they stood at the ready on the balls of their feet. No sign of guns, but there were bulges at the ankles and one had brass knuckles kissing the fingers of his right hand.

Not a pedestrian in sight. The natives knew when to get lost. Not the first occurrence, then. Only people who ran a town could flout the potential for violence so easily. Sure, explained why that one-woman big brass band of a waitress looked like she'd seen Sasquatch molesting her poodle when I showed her Canton's pic.

Five against one. Bad odds, but I'd faced worse. Only one thing to do.

The leader took an overhand right to the nose, which

squelched against my knuckles, breaking messily in a shower of blood and snot. I spun as number two realized this wasn't going as planned and smashed his jaw with an elbow. Teeth flew, clattering on the concrete. Number three actually drew his gun before my underhand throw left a knife in his thigh. He screamed.

A pistol discharged in my ear, sending a burning wire through my auditory canal and I gave number four a knee to the gonads as I screamed in pain. A punch to me butt cheek sent me stumbling, but I managed to trip up number one as he swung at me, mouth red and screaming from his gushing schnozz.

Time to go. My feet took off and my body followed while my butt felt like burning coals had been inserted under the muscles, but adrenalin does wonders, the fear of soon to be departed bodily parts better than a slug of rye on a cold day.

Eyes watering, the back of my legs warm liquid … trouble running, but I managed a stumble stutter that ate up the distance. From behind came shouts, warning to stop but [DELETE] that noise, no way. Why do the cops and bad guys always yell for the ones they're chasing to stop? Oh, please mister victim/criminal, let me do terrible things to your tender flesh, all you have to do is stand still like a good little moron.

A juke to the right then a hard left down an alley, hot yellow spots in my vision and sweat streaming down my legs into my shoes just as someone punched me in the ass once again. Should have worn Nikes or Reeboks instead of Eccos. Silly me. Next time, yeah, next time I'll do better.

Getting old, forgetful. Didn't prep well enough. Should have showed up with a team, not have one shadow me. Man, I felt like a major bonehead.

A gem filled my palm, a beryl. "CHINFLINT!" I yelled, tossing it over my shoulder. A puff as black smoke filled the alley behind. Good old spell gems. Just what the doctor ordered. Things were looking up.

Almost to the end of the alley, I could see a street empty of cars. My butt was killing me, harsh hard pain in both cheeks that made me want to weep. Soon. I'd get away soon and re-group, get my bearings and find those fake-tatted douchebags and give them a good old Hakala beatdown, not just because they deserved it but because they probably had a clue as to Canton's whereabouts. I let that thought take my mind from the pain.

The damn cargo van appeared as if by magic, screech-ing to a halt, the douchebags boiling out like clowns out of a Fiat and I threw another spell gem almost by reflex, yelling, "WIMPLEWOMPLE!"

Really? Wimplewomple? Special Branch must've been hard up for activation words. Still, the spell grenade cooked off quite well and two of the douchebags blew apart in a red mist as the report and concussion blew me back into the alley, my ears a ringing mess. I landed on my ass.

I screamed. Someone had taken an egg beater and was shredding my *gluteus maximus* at high speed. Looking down I saw the sweat lining my pants was really blood and I felt the world tilt a bit.

The douchebag leader appeared, Taser in hand, a rather unhappy expression on his pug ugly face.

"You shot me in the ass!" I yelled in disbelief.

He pulled the trigger and I experienced a 50,000-volt Jitterbug.

CHAPTER SIX

Canton

Somewhere Else

C*RACK!*
Razor hot agony lit my back again and I screamed, no longer able to keep my cool.

Crack!

Fire and blood, salty sweat in open wounds. My back arched, and my stomach scraped stained wood, punching splinters into my abdomen.

Crack!

How did it get to be so bad? Blood coated my teeth and tongue. The inside of my cheeks had been chewed to bits.

***

Two months ago:

I CAME TO ON A cot made of rough-planed wood and coarse woolen fibers that were too scratchy for comfort. One second asleep, or I thought I was, the next utter, complete awareness of the world all around. Small room, more of a cell. Iron bars made one wall, rough stone the others.

The smell. That doggone smell. Feces, urine, sweat and blood mixed together with rotting straw and halitosis.

No confusion this time. No worries, no 'where the hell am I' because I knew by the primitive conditions and the thread-bare breechclout I wore I still remained in the past somewhen. In fact, I had a pretty good doggone idea when I was.

First century BC, Roman Empire. I could feel it like the slimy air that slithered into my lungs, the fetor of human hope-lessness and misery, of violence and hate.

I stood in one fluid motion, unhurt by smashed ribs or torn skin … all the damage done by Aeneas erased from my flesh. Doggone it, I felt good.

Hair cut close to the skull, an inch all the way around. Scars, but all the old ones from years at the Bureau like the long one on my shoulder from the lamia in Wisconsin and the ragged burn from a salamander in Maine. Nothing new.

A narrow hallway seen dimly through bars, the fitful light of an oil lamp adding to the stink. The floor rotting straw, no doubt filled with fleas. My feet covered in crude leather sandals.

"Three," I breathed. "Two, one …"

On cue a voice barked down the hallway, "Cantor, your reward is here."

More light. A torch spitting shadows. A big man gone to fat, gelatinous belly overlapping a leather kilt arrived leading a woman in a soiled loincloth. A familiar face. I knew the name.

"Claudia," I said. Not Talya, although she wore the same face. Claudia, a Roman name for a Roman woman. A Roman slave. How did I know all this?

She looked at me, brown eyes so big they eclipsed her face like one of those Manga cartoons. The fat man rattled keys and opened the door to the cell, shoving her in. "Good job in the arena, Gladiator," he humphed. "My lord was pleased at the sport you provided."

Gladiator. Yes. I knew that. Unlike the previous incarnation at Troy, I had memories of an entire life, the life of a Carthaginian warrior captured in battle and sold into slavery. Of arriving in Capua filthy and exhausted, open sores scoring my back and feet and being inspected like the piece of livestock I was and not being able to do anything about it. As I stared at the woman who stared back at me, it all came crashing down, the memories of this inherited life. Perhaps all the weird stuff I'd encountered as an agent inured me to the oddity of this situation because I was remarkably okay with everything. Sure, I was pissed that someone tucked me into the ass end of history but rolling with the punches was all part of the job.

We were left alone, us two. I stared at Claudia, not able to tear my eyes away. So beautiful, so young. More than the girl she'd been at Troy. Yet there was something familiar beyond our connection to each other, a sense of déjà vu that had the back of my brain itching fiercely.

"Who are you, Claudia," I whispered. "Or is it Talya?"

Eyes downcast. "Claudia, my lord. I know not this Talya you speak of."

"Why are you here?" I searched my memory. This was the second time Cantor had seen Claudia; she was a house slave in the main quarters of the *dominus* of this *ludus*. The master, or owner, of this gladiator school.

She looked puzzled, but said, "I am your prize for winning your bout against the Greek Euchalos the Fierce." That said, she closed the distance between us and placed soft arms around my shoulders. It felt like a homecoming.

As her lips met mine, all thoughts and reservations disappeared.

**

CRACK!

Oh god, my back hurt, my throat hurt, my stomach hurt.

Everything hurt but it just kept on coming and there wasn't a doggone thing I could do.

Crack!

***

One day ago:

"ALL RIGHT, MAGGOTS, PUT YOUR backs into it. My grand-mother can hoist sand better than that!" The *doctore's* voice cracked as hard a whip, cutting through the air easily. A slave, the *doctore* was our trainer, a veteran gladiator given semi-retirement as a teacher.

This particular human possessed all the mean of every DI I'd ever encountered and then a good patch more. Scarred with only one ear and a mashed-up excuse of a nose, his horrifying looks masked a horrifying personality that was composed of equal parts malice, hatred and disgust at anything and anyone that wasn't him.

I lifted the forty-pound sack of sand and threw it seven feet toward my training partner, Crixus. My shoulders ached as the primitive medicine ball left my hands, sending a twinge down my back. Crixus caught the sack easily and tossed it back like a tennis ball, his casual strength almost awe inspiring to watch. Big across the shoulders, long arms and short, bandy legs, the Gallic warrior looked more at home as a gladiator than I felt.

"Tired, Cantor?" he asked with a gap-toothed grin. Through the backstory I knew that he'd taken me in when I first arrived, guiding me through the slave society of the brutal *ludus* and the sadistic *doctore* who ruled over us all with the iron hand of a dictator.

I hurled the leather-clad ball of sand back. Ouch, that hurt. "No," I panted.

"Liar."

"How can you tell?"

A wooden rod smacked me in the back of the legs and I fell, hamstrings stunned by the sting.

The *doctore* stood over me with a fierce scowl. Not that that deviated from his normal hate-filled, expression. "No talking!" he screamed, spittle flying.

For a moment I wanted to go all Krav Maga on his ass, but that might earn me a quick crucifixion. Romans weren't known for being all cuddly and warm to lawbreakers. Especially slave lawbreakers.

All around the fifteen-foot walls of the *ludus* sheltered the Roman citizens of Capua from the sight of brutal gladiatorial training. Here and there were stains, dried crusty ones, that told of unfortunate slaves who felt the wrath of the *dominus*, Gnaeus Cornelius Lentulus Batiatus, who currently occupied a spot in what I called the owner's box, a small covered balcony attached to the main house overlooking the *ludus*.

Not fat, not thin, the *lanista* (a person who owned and trained gladiators) Batiatus reclined on a couch, goblet of wine in hand, staring down at forty or so slave gladiators sweating their asses off. Mine included. He looked bored and not inclined to interfere with the *doctore's* discipline.

"Get your maggoty butt out of the dirt!" screamed the *doctore*, spittle flying from his lips.

I stood. "Yes, *doctore*." Any other response was met by the whip coiled at his side. I towered over the smaller man, but even though he was out of shape and running to fat, I had a feeling he could punch a hole in my chest and rip out my still-beating heart.

"I can't figure you out, Cantor." The hate never left his scarred face despite lowering his voice, so I barely caught the words. Nearby, Crixus strained to eavesdrop. "You've been here all of three weeks, fairly competent with a gladius." This was an enormous compliment. Such praise rarely left those twisted, ugly lips. "A soldier, a killer, and a gladiator, yet you hesitate to kill in the arena. Why is that? Why would such a Carthaginian slayer hesitate to kill gladiators and criminals in the arena?"

He wasn't expecting an answer, but I gave him one anyway. "Just because I'm good at killing doesn't mean I like it."

I didn't see the fist that took me in the gut, he was that fast.

Eating dirt, trying not to vomit. Sweat and tears in my eyes, the laughter of a few dozen hard men in my ears. A knot of hot agony twisting in my abdomen forcing my lungs closed and black spots in my eyes told me that oxygen was a scarce commodity in my flesh.

Suddenly my lungs started working and cool air hit them in a rush that had me dizzy in an instant. I almost cried with relief.

The *doctore's* evil voice slithered into my ears. "Listen to me, maggot. You are the property of Gnaeus Cornelius Lentulus Batiatus, the greatest *dominus* of the greatest *ludus* in all of the Empire, you remember that. The fact that the *dominus* himself purchased you from Crassus the slave trader is remarkable because the *dominus* hates Crassus so much that the mere sight of that flea bitten, mule-eyed whoreson is an offense to his patrician sensibilities. He saw something in you, Cantor, something hard and mean and vicious, so he bought you and sent you into the arena almost immediately without any training. That you won against that scrofulous Greek merely illuminates the *dominus'* great ability to judge the worthiness of a potential gladiator. You are the second such specimen to show up in the space of a month with such potential."

Here the vile trainer leaned in even closer. The smell of rotting teeth brought nausea to my stomach. He needed extra-strength Listerine. "You were a soldier, you killed only when necessary upon the orders of your officers. You stood behind a shield and used a xiphos, or javelin or falcate ... whatever weapon you whoresons used and relied on your brothers at your side to protect your flanks. Here, however, you're a gladiator. No brothers except for those of the house of Batiatus. You fight for only one purpose: to kill. No exceptions. If you do not fight, you die. If you do not train every day, you die. If you do not follow every order as if it were produced by the mouth of

Jupiter himself, you die. There are no alternatives, no choices. A slave you are and a slave you'll die unless you earn the *Rudis*, the wooden sword symbolizing freedom, given to exceptional gladiators for years of outstanding combat. There is no other way ... the *Rudis* or through the gates into Dis Pater's realm. My coin is on the god of the Underworld." The rotting breath receded, and I was given a kick in the ass. "Get up."

I got up. Half the dusty training ground was crusted to my sweaty legs and chest.

"Come, Cantor, the *dominus* wishes to talk."

What the *dominus* wanted, he got.

The center of the house was an open courtyard filled with potted flowers of every variety and color, jasmine, crocus, bluebells, periwinkles, geraniums, oleanders, convolvulus and aquilegia. The smell sure beat the odor of the slave pens by a goodly patch. Scantily clad slave women in iron collars and threadbare, but clean, tunics tended the garden, watering and pruning as necessary and, like the flowers, were chosen for their beauty. I could have stared at the floral overload for days but the last slave, a gnarled man almost my height, jarred with the scene.

Scarred, wide, large hands and feet, he had a palm-sized burn mark on his neck where the flesh ran like wax. Hate and anger flared from his gray eyes and I fancied I could feel the heat. He wore a gladiator's breechclout and thick manacles on his wrists.

"Cantor." The *dominus* flowed into the courtyard, certain of his mastery over all within, a goblet of wine in hand and dressed top to bottom in a plain white toga made of wool. He motioned me to sit on a nearby stone couch. I did so gratefully.

Beady brown eyes regarded me intensely. "There is not another gladiator that hates you, Cantor. Why is that?"

Sarcasm with the *dominus* would get me the lash, so I answered quickly and honestly. "My time here will be better if I make no enemies, so I go out of my way to be ... agreeable."

Laughter. "Smart. Smarter than the normal Carthaginian

soldier-turned-slave. You assessed the situation and adapted. Just like in the arena against that Greek. You didn't know how to handle a sica, so you used your speed and shield to batter the man unconscious. It was such a show that *Propraetor* Lupus, visiting from Rome, spared the defeated man's life. He offered to purchase you, but I know good flesh when I see it and I saw something in you that day I haven't seen in a while." Batiatus leaned in close. "I saw a survivor." To the *doctore*. "Correct, yes?"

A nod. Even around the *dominus* his face was still a mask of hate and distain. "No one in Capua or the Empire can match your eye for potential, *dominus*."

Mouth shut and eyes straight ahead. Batiatus wasn't looking for conversation, but affirmation.

Survival. That was the game.

Batiatus held his goblet out and a servant appeared out of the foliage with an ewer. Claudia.

The *dominus* followed my eyes. "Claudia, eh? A fine specimen. As fine as I've ever owned. Come here child." He lightly grasped her chin between thumb and forefinger. "Do I know good stock or do I? She is a prize, one that I give to those who please me, like you Cantor. But now I will give her to the *doctore* as a present on the fifth anniversary of his position here in my *ludus*."

I couldn't help it, my emotions were raw and right on my sleeve. My body tensed before I could stop myself and Batiatus caught it.

"Ah, you have feelings for the woman?"

No reply.

He gave me a look I'd seen plenty of times and I nodded, not trusting my voice.

"You want me to keep her from the *doctore*?"

Here I thought I didn't have a weak spot. Just goes to show that life has a way of throwing a curveball that'll knock your socks off. "Yes, *dominus*."

"No way that will happen," said the *doctore*. "What the

dominus wills, it is made real." A scarred hand rose and caressed Claudia's breast through her rough tunic.

One second seated, the next my hands reached, the *doctore* stumbling back in surprise. The soft *shiiiing* of a gladii leaving sheaths and I was surrounded by plate wearing guards with blades drawn and murder in their eyes. I had completely forgotten about my escort of house guards.

As for Batiatus, he was *laughing*. "Wonderful!" He clapped his hands and the four guards retreated, although the swords didn't see the inside of their sheaths. "Do you know the first rule of training a gladiator, Cantor? Find a way to control them, give them a reason to fight for you, to fight to *win*. That is why my *ludus* is the best in all the Empire, I know what each and every one of my gladiator's desire." The *dominus* took a long sip of wine and I felt the hard itch at the back of my throat as I stared at the goblet. My mouth was dust dry. "Crixus desires money, to gamble upon his bouts in the arena, and I allow him to do so and buy trinkets for his favorite whores. For Landolf, I allow him a cell filled with luxuries he fights very hard to maintain, knowing that it could be stripped away from him at any time.

"And do you see this brute of a Thracian?" Batiatus laid a hand on the slave with the burned neck. If looks could kill, the *dominus* would've caught fire right then and there. "He has a fighting spirit this one, but he doesn't talk much. Doesn't even talk to the other slaves, preferring to keep to himself in his little cell, but I know what he wants, Cantor, and I will use it to make him a fighter these shores haven't seen since Aeneas landed here centuries ago. What do you think?"

"What is his desire, *dominus*?" I asked.

"Freedom. This man wishes to be free, all he wants is to return to his clan, the Maedi, so I will offer him the *Rudis* when he wins fifty fights in the arena. With this passion for freedom, he will fight, and he will kill."

A chill went down my spine. I had me a bad feeling. "Who is he, *dominus*?"

"I don't know. He won't say his name. No threat of flogging will loosen his tongue. Perhaps you should name him. Something noble, something fierce and war-like. What do you say, Cantor? Care to give this man a proud Carthaginian name?"

The Thracian glared. He did it well. I knew this man. Not personally, but from history and a popular television series. It seemed that time or whoever had decided to drop my butt into some of the most historically significant times in Western culture. I shook my head. "No, *dominus*, he deserves a proud Thracian name. Call him Spartacus."

For the first time the scarred man smiled, and it chilled me to the bone.

CHAPTER SEVEN

Kal

———•———

A Pain In The …

OUCH. MEGA OUCH. OUCH with a side of agony sauce and pain fries.

Rumbling. Rambling. Thumps and bumps and an uneven vibration. What happened? Last thing I remembered was fighting, using spell gems, then …

…doing the jelly dance while a zillion volts passed through me. Oh yeah. That I remember. My head thrummed with every thump and bump and all I could do was keep my eyes closed and let blessed darkness comfort me.

"How long?" A rough voice full of phlegm. A smoker, if I had a guess.

"We'll get there when we get there." A second voice, one I recognized belonging to the leader of the faux-tat club.

"This guy had more hardware on him than Home Depot. Garrotes, punch knives, guns, and that funky leather belt of his, I mean [CENSORED] me! It turns into a damn sword! About had a heart attack when I checked it out. He killed Donal and Hecks. Man, there wasn't enough of them to scrape up off the sidewalk. Did you see that spell gem cook? I've never seen anything like it."

"I have," stated the leader flatly. "Wylie himself executed a traitor two years ago. Boiled his brains inside the guy's skull until they shot out the ears and eyes. Sickest damn thing I've ever seen."

"[REDACTED] magicians."

"You can say that again."

"[REDACTED] magicians."

Bunch of comedians. Fantastic. I lay there, letting the thumps and bumps and noise wash over me while I assessed. So far, I learned a couple of things:

I was lying on the floor of that cargo van, one of the only non-commercial vehicles that could easily accommodate a specimen of my size and not be conspicuous. I could clearly hear the road noise. Probably the same van the fake-tat boys used.

These guys were definitely only semi-professional and, considering the nature of Canton's mission, probably members of that organization we busted in Omaha.

These bozos weren't SEAL trained, but there were more of them and my ass hurt.

My ass hurt. So much. That's what all the ouching was about. These guys shot me in the damn ass!

***

IT WAS TIME TO PLAY dead. Or at least extremely unconscious. Sometimes the only way out is through. I let the pain ride over me and kept my ears tuned to radio fake-tat. In just a few short minutes my patience was rewarded.

"What do you think Mr. Q is going to do with this Bureau guy?"

The leader took a moment before answering. "I just told you the brain boiling story, didn't I?"

Laughter.

Not from me, though. I was fresh out. Put brain boiling down at the top of the list of 'Most Horrible Ways To Die' under bored to death by a congressional hearings. Talk about a cruel and unusual punishment.

It seemed I had a date with a Magician. Definitely from that criminal organization that went undetected for years. Selling kids with the magic gene to the highest bidder was the most heinous of their crimes. Believe me, I'd read the dossier on them and they actually made Satan look like a parish priest. Nothing made me happier than doing those creeps dirty when I discovered one of their cells in Omaha.

After the Omaha op (it involved my least-favorite Supernatural ... vampires), the various Bureaus around the world went a-huntin' waskally wabbits, but unlike Elmer Fudd, they were much, much better at the job. The organization was virtually wiped out within a matter of months.

Virtually. Unfortunately, it looked like we didn't turn over enough rocks and now it looked like one of the wabbits had Canton, and me.

Fantastic.

After a few minutes of casual conversation between my brainiac captors, the van slowed and came to a stop.

"Grab this piece of [DELETED], Ham. He's too big for me to carry."

"He's still leaking."

"Two slugs in the butt will do that to you."

"Bet it hurts worse than living with my ex-wife."

"That ain't [CENSORED] possible."

Yeah, that's the humor I had to put up with. They acted more like frat boys getting ready to steal the other team's mascot rather than two professionals, but that was hunky dory with me because I needed them not to be Johnny-on-the-spot, so I could do them some serious hurt soon.

Large hands grabbed my shoulders and legs and the metal-lic rumble of a sliding van door assaulted my ears. Up and out into fading sunlight. My butt cheeks screamed as the wounds opened and I chewed a hole in my tongue in an effort to remain silent. I felt my consciousness slip, slip, slipping away and I fought it with every ounce of discipline and plain old Finnish stubbornness in my body.

"Jesus this guy weighs a ton."

"These Bureau types always do."

"Yeah, remember that Indian dude? Not as tall, but he was all muscle."

Canton!

Pain forgotten, I was all desperate emotion instead and I spun out of the hands holding me, not worrying about bleeding or magicians or hitting concrete enough to bruise my ribs. I opened my eyes and kicked out, my shoe connecting with a *crunch* that bent a knee the wrong way.

A scream, some cursing. A shoe came at me and I grabbed it, heaving, using all of my might and twisting the foot 180 degrees. A sickening pop and more screaming. Two men on the ground and me suddenly on my feet facing another fake-tat bad guy who looked angry enough to eat nails and crap staples. He went for a straight jab to the nose, fast enough to connect to my cheek, which exploded in some fresh pain, but I was seeing three shades of red and I wasn't going to stop until I got what I came for, which was my best friend and I punched my anger at the third man, putting the length of my body into the blow and his jaw went sideways, losing teeth and I hit him again, not raging, no … the rage, the warlike magic that fueled me for ten years was long gone, gone with my sister's spirit into the other world, the world of the dead, but I still had plenty of mad going on, good old fashioned anger and it fueled me enough to hit the guy again and again until his head spun about and his neck *cracked* like well-dried wishbone and he fell lifeless among the writhing bodies of his pals and I stood there, breathing hard and reining back the fury that made me want to stomp a hole in the survivors.

The leader, the one grasping his knee in apparent agony,

babbled a mixture of curses, threat and pleas, but they didn't stop me one bit from grabbing a good hunk of black hair and I half-lifted him to his feet. He made with some more scream-ing, but I wasn't feeling all lovey dovey because this poor excuse of a clump of used toilet paper didn't deserve a shred of mercy. The small bit of me that still held on to all his marbles screamed at me to stop, but I drowned it out with a chorus of '*Bad to the Bone.*'

Funny what your mind dredges up when sanity is in the rear view.

"Okay, Mr. Fake Tattoo man," I growled, my nose an inch from his. "Where is Canton Alsate?"

I could tell he didn't want to say anything, but he was in no condition to put up a fuss. "Who?"

"The Native American guy you snatched."

A blank look.

"The Indian, you nitwit."

The oldest trick in the book is to look over your oppo-nent's shoulder at some other potential threat or ally swiftly approaching. Mr. Fake Tattoo went for it, but I wasn't buying.

Stupid me.

And here is where things went all wiggly again.

***

An undetermined time later:

NO WAKING UP IN A van. This time it was a bed, a soft one that seemed pretty comfy, in fact. It took a few seconds for my vision to clear, but when it did I saw I was in a decent-sized room, about fifteen-by-fifteen with the bed smack in the middle.

My ankles and wrists hurt. I wiggled them and discovered handcuffs. Plastic ties and the traditional metal. Turned out that the bed I lay in was a sturdy mission style, oak and heavy as hell no doubt. I gave my restraints a fierce tug. The bed didn't budge. Yep, sturdy. As for the rest of me, the only thing that separated me from the bedsheets was the thin cotton of my boxers.

Fantastic. At least they left me underwear. I craned my head around. No other furniture and the window was boarded with one-by-fours, the late-afternoon sunlight slithering in almost vertically. Not too much time passed, then, unless it was twenty-four hours later than, yes, far too much.

Strange thing, though … no pain in my ass. No damage whatsoever. For me to have healed so quickly meant magic, and magic meant a magician. Someone wanted me to be tiptop when they started working me over. That cut the odds a little bit in my favor despite the circumstances.

Now, waking up finding yourself handcuffed and zip-tied to a bed that looked like it had been assembled by big, beefy, lederhosen-wearing, dark beer chugging, over muscled German craftsman might induce a state of panic. For the normal agent, it would.

I left normal in the rear view a looooong time ago.

So, it was with an eerie sense of calm I waited for the inevitable arrival of the bad guy. I could've written this script in my sleep.

There he was. I had to give him style points … one second not there, the next *there*. While there's no such thing as an invisibility spell (some physical laws have yet to be bent that far) there are spells that affect the mind, causing a sort of situational blindness where the presence of the leering arch-villain doesn't register in your visual cortex. Pretty cool, actually.

"So, what do we have here?" said Mr. Villain. Darn it … he didn't have a long mustache to twirl. It would have been so cool if he fit that stereotype, a sort of Snidely Whiplash from *Dudley Do-Right*.

If he was waiting for me to scream in alarm, he had another think coming. I gave him the old hairy eyeball and kept my mouth shut.

A shade over six feet and out of shape, Mr. Villain leaned over. "Who are you?"

"I'm the bloke what's gonna do you right, ain't I?"

He rolled his crap brown eyes. "Oh, lord. MI-7." The name of UK's version of the Bureau. "What brings you to American soil?"

"Well now, that's none of your business, is it Nosey Parker?"

His rather round face turned vinegar sour. "You are an agent, highly trained, but I am a magician." Said with immense gravitas, he waited for me to look impressed or afraid. When my face remained impassive, Mr. Villain straightened the cuffs of his black three piece and continued his bad guy monologue. "Understand that you are our prisoner. We know that you came for the Native American Bureau Agent, Canton Alsate." At least he didn't say Indian, give him credit for that. "But you must have information … information about Bureau activity in Talladega, teams assigned and such."

Mouth shut time. Give him the old silent treatment. Soon now. I tried not to smile.

"Tell me about your mission, the disposition of your teams." More silence. This was easy.

No sign of irritation yet from Mr. Villain. "Okay. I understand You don't want to be a traitor to those you fight with. I understand. Really, I do. And I have not given you any reason to trust me, to take me at my word. I understand that as well. No guarantee of a *quid quo pro*. Very reasonable on your part. Like you, I am a reasonable man, I know how to dangle the carrot and the stick.

"The carrot, so to speak, in this scenario, is your life. I will scrub all memory of this encounter from your mind without harming your other faculties, so if you cooperate, you have nothing to fear. You will simply wake up in the restroom of a truck stop near Birmingham with a slight headache and no clue as to how you came to be there. Simple. All you have to do, and it really is the easiest of all things, is to impart upon me one teeny, tiny bit of information. Nothing about your team, or teams. Nothing about the inner workings of the Bureau, we already have that information, and not a word about any deep dark secret you may harbor in your soul."

Had to hand it to him, it was a good pitch. Really top notch. "And what do I have drop into your delicate shell-like, mate? What secret has your knickers in a twist, then?"

"All you have to tell me, Mr. Whoever you are because your name sure isn't what's on this phony driver's license, is the current whereabouts and disposition of one Kalevi Hakala."

There it was. With a solid click the last piece fell into place and suddenly I knew down to lower intestine what this whole mess was about ... the sighting of the ninja assassin chick, sending Canton down and his subsequent kidnapping and the disappearance of the team shadowing him. Everything.

It was to get to me.

Sonofabitch, could they ever hold a grudge. Just because I discovered and helped bring down their criminal enterprise, *I'm* the bad guy ...

"What makes you think I know what's with that geezer? I have different things occupying me attention, mate. As far as I know, Hakala is sitting on his bum in the Bureau compound."

"Wrong!" thundered the magician in a sudden burst of rage like a bolt of lightning out of the clear blue. "Don't lie to me," he hissed, bending over me and giving with the stink eye. His face was bloated and red like a brick. "Never lie to me. I know he's on assignment, I know he's in Alabama and I want him."

Just as quickly as he was to anger, suddenly he stood, patting his hair to make sure it was in place. "Now, you will tell me, and you will be set free, or you will tell me after I do things to you that the Marquis de Sade couldn't even *believe*."

I didn't know about the Marquis, but I sure believed all right, but I had me a plan. Only problem was how much I wanted to poke the bear. Hmmm ... let's see ... "Gov, how about you kiss me arse and then have your wife come in and let me kiss hers? Sounds good to me, don't it?"

Yeah, that worked. Mr. Villain was used to people cringing

at his every word, a bully's wet dream. No doubt he was surrounded by those who wouldn't even let the idea of a cross thought about the boss enter their tiny pea brains. That made my defiance and insults sting even more, like I hoped.

A flabby forearm found its way hard against my throat, almost choking my wind. "Do you have any *idea* of what I want to do to you? Do you understand the pain and the horror that's mine to command with just a simple look?"

There it was. I grinned.

Mr. Villain snarled, "What are you grinning about, you fool? Your nanolocator has been disabled and there's no one to hear you scream."

The nanolocator, the tiny tracking device injected into my butt cheek. Either the bullet or the magician put paid to the Bureau's ability to find me, but I had me a plan, I did, and a good one at that.

"You're still grinning." Mr. Villain vomited the words as if they hurt his stomach. "Why are you still grinning? You're no magician, you have no hope."

Wrong, Mr. Villain, I thought with manic glee. On both counts.

I won't go into the whole I-was-really-supposed-to-be-a-magician-but-my-sister-attached-her-soul-to-mine-and-put-the-kibosh-on-that-career-choice thing. Long story and not germane except that I *was* a magician. Not a good one. Not a powerful one. Actually, I possessed only one spell in my repertoire and that turned to be the weakest one of all. The Zippo spell.

Looking into those crap-brown eyes, I reached down deep for every bit of anger and hate and desperation I could muster, every emotion that clamored to be released in an orgy of chaotic destruction. The desire to live, to smash this idiot's brains in with a shovel, to tear and rend and howl my fury at the moon drove the magic from deep within in a roaring torrent because I needed everything in me, everything I was to do what I planned. Something I didn't think possible. Maybe it wasn't but I was sure as little green apples going to give it a serious try.

"What are you doing?" Mr. Villain shouted in my face. Why didn't the bad guys ever invest in breath mints?

No answer from me, I was trying to give with the mojo and I could feel it rushing upward like lava from the core of the earth. *There!* The magic, a heady feeling, a better rush than pot or alcohol with none of the downtime. I could see the spell Shape in my mind, the elegant, yet simple, a three-dimensional magical equation of the Zippo spell, ready to call forth a quarter-sized lick of fire that would last for about ten seconds.

I needed more. Much more. I put my will to it, my mental shoulder to the magical grindstone and pulled more energy into the Shape, more and more and more because I had me a plan, a plan to do that Mr. Villain bloke a big nasty and I needed all the juice I could get. More and more and more, my forehead broke out in sweat and it felt like my eyeballs would pop out of the sockets and lay on my cheeks, dangling from the string of the optic nerves.

"WHAT ARE YOU DOING!" screamed the magician. The forearm dug in my throat, but I was way too far gone to feel it. I didn't need air, didn't need anything but the sweet release of spell casting.

The Shape revolved slowly in my mental sight, trim and perfect, pregnant with purpose. It looked ripe and ready to go, but I needed something more, something I'd never done before, never *heard* done before.

I split the Shape in two. The tearing at my mind hurt so much and I felt a trickle from my nose as I bit my lip. The Shapes, sparkling and halved, revolved around their severed axis and began to reform as agony threatened to shatter my sanity into a thousand sparkling needles of crystal.

Two Shapes. Two spells cast at the same time instead of one. Grinning savagely, lips and tongue torn by my teeth, I spat at Mr. Villain and *pushed* the spells out.

CHAPTER EIGHT

Canton

———•———

Whip it Good

CRACK!

Fire ate my skin and blood spattered onto thirsty dirt. All around me the other gladiators watched.

Crack!

Throat raw, I had no more breath or capacity to scream. All my screams were gone, fled my neck long since. Nothing to do but hang there by rough, iron manacles and bleed.

Crack!

***

One day ago:

"SPARTACUS, EH?" BATIATUS STROKED HIS CHIN. "There was a king in Thrace by that name, if I recall. I like it."

All I could do there was stare dumbly. Spartacus, the man who sparked a slave revolt that shook the Roman Empire to its roots. While the legions fought in the Third Mithriadatic War and a revolt in Spain, Spartacus' ragtag army scoured the countryside, picking up more and more raw recruits, escaped slaves, who saw their chance to be free. All doomed to fail.

Maybe I could change that.

Just by being here I'd disrupted the future. Maybe I could disrupt it some more. I knew some of the history of Rome and the Third Servile War. Just enough to alter the outcome, give the slaves a fighting chance.

"What do you think, *doctore*?" Batiatus asked the overseer. "Do you like the name Spartacus?"

"Whatever the *dominus* desires," came the impassive reply. His eyes were practically raping Claudia. I felt my fists tighten.

Batiatus noticed. "I can grant your desire, Cantor. But only if you earn it."

"Dominus?"

The owner of the *ludus* turned toward the overseer, who snapped to attention. "Can you defeat this man?" Batiatus asked.

A nod. "Easily, *dominus*."

"Good, *doctore*, good." When Batiatus turned back to me, the smile on his face was far from pleasant and I felt a chill squirm around in my gut. "You two shall fight." He raised a finger. "But not to the death. If you win, I will give you Claudia right here, right now. If the *doctore* wins, I will make a gift of her to him until such time as you win your third match in the arena. Yes, that sounds fair. I think it will be so."

I stood. "All I have to do is beat him, *dominus*?"

Again, that unpleasant smile. "Yes, of course."

Fast. Faster than I'd ever moved before. Batiatus, Claudia, the guards and the fragrant garden became a blur, the only clear image was the *doctore*, eyes widening in surprise, hand moving in slow motion toward the whip at his belt, all the malice in his homely face turning to fear as I closed the distance and I wanted to hurt him, doggone *needed* to hurt him something awful for the way he touched Claudia, for putting his filthy hands on her body in such an intimate, yet horrifying, way

and that wasn't going to fly in my book, no sir, because a man
is supposed to care for the weak, the strong are supposed to be
defenders, dammit, but too often they go from caretakers to
just plain takers.

As fast as I went (I thought I could feel the air sizzle across
my skin) the *doctore* managed to react with a hard left toward
my skull, but he was just a gladiator, a mere killer. Me, I was
an *agent*.

My fingers found themselves laced around his wrist and I
turned, raising my shoulder while whipping that arm down.
A hard impact across my deltoid and the *doctore's* elbow bent
the wrong way, the bone snapping with a report like a gunshot.

He screamed. I didn't stop. Both clavicles and a couple of
ribs popped as I put paid to his indecent lechery and the next
thing I knew as the man screamed liked his throat was about
to collapse was just about every Roman soldier in the Empire
landed on me hard, dragging me into darkness.

I smiled just before something hard and metallic to the
back of my skull sent me away.

***

"YOUR ENTHUSIASM TO BEST MY *doctore* has earned you this,"
Batiatus remarked, breath reeking of wine. "He is of no use to
me now. The *medicus* tells me he will never be the same, that
even if he recovers fully, he will be crippled and cannot serve
me to train a new generation of gladiators."

The wooden post dug into my chest, the chains held my
wrists tight, dragging me to my tiptoes. I could've climbed
the rough pole, but the guards stationed around the training
yard knew their duty and were fixing to turn me into an acu-
puncture Apache in a moment's notice should I get up to any
shenanigans.

"*Dominus*, I did not kill him, as was instructed." I kept my
eyes averted. No need to play dominance games with a man

who had me chained to a post in the middle of the *ludus*. "You didn't say anything about maiming him."

That earned me a scowl. "Twenty lashes, Cantor. It will hurt. It will be pain like you've never felt in your misbegotten life, but you can strive through and win out the other end. I will see you healed, I will see you a champion the likes of which will shake the very foundations of Rome and when you make me one of the richest men in the empire, I will honor you with the *Rudis*."

I held my tongue, knowing doggone well that I'd be using it like all get-out soon enough.

Batiatus withdrew and Crixus took his place. "I am sorry, Cantor, but I have been selected as the new *doctore* and must administer the whip."

"Do what you have to," I replied, spotting Claudia out of the corner of my eye. Her face was pinched and swollen as if she'd been crying. "If you're caught going easy on me, it'll be you against this post."

He placed his ham hand on my shoulder and squeezed before disappearing from view, leaving only the crowd and Claudia in my vision. I heard him uncoil the whip, a slithery, creaky sound, and twirl it experimentally.

The crowd drew a collective breath.

Crack!

***

SWEAT STUNG MY EYES, NOT as bad as the whip stung my hide, but annoying all the same. The roaring in my ears drowned out the bloodlust of the gladiators and Claudia's cries. My back felt like fire licked at it, eating away fat and muscle, going in deep for bone and my lungs felt full of broken glass, the jagged edges tearing at my raw flesh.

"Hold!" No more crack of the whip. My cheek scraped

against the rough and dirty pole as tears streamed down my face, carving through dust and stubble.

Batiatus' face appeared, inches away. His breath smelled of bad wine and garlic. "You have been punished enough, slave. Now it is time to make of you a champion."

My vision swam and the fire on my back threatened to consume me. *So doggone tired. So doggone hurt.* I blinked. "What?"

"A champion. You, along with that brute Spartacus. You will make me rich and in return I will make you free. All you must do is surrender to my will. The pain will stop, and you will heal and begin a new phase in your life." That wine breath curdled the acid in my stomach. "Do you surrender, Cantor?"

I turned my head, rubbing skin against the dirty post and looked at the crowd of gladiators. Some were watching like this was reality TV, and some looked on horrified, casting their glances up and down, but never at the red ruin of my back.

There …

Claudia. A tear dribbled down her cheek and I tried to smile. It hurt. She cut back a sob, eyes crinkling in sorrow.

"No."

"Excuse me? What?"

I turned my head back to Batiatus. "No."

"No? What do you mean no? You're a slave, that precludes you from saying no. You have no will, no self-direction. No more than a horse because you are property." Anger flared in his soft eyes. "Now submit to my will. This is an order from your *dominus.*"

"No." Easier this time. The word sailed out loud and hard.

Batiatus flinched. "Submit!"

"No."

"Submit your will to me or you will suffer so, endure such pain as you cannot *imagine.* This is your owner, your *dominus,* greatest *lanista* of the greatest *ludus* in Rome speaking and you will do as I command. There is no other alternative."

"No."

Face white with fury, Batiatus grabbed me by both ears and

knocked my head against the post and the world became all shiny colors and stars.

But inside there was peace, a sort of pervasive contentment as I stuck to my decision. The road had been taken, the first step behind and no matter what came, I could die happy. My will was my own, not a thing to be used by vulgar men and if that meant a serious boat load of pain, well then, so be it.

"Whip him! Whip him until I can see the beating of his heart! I want this man dead within the hour."

Sweat added salty agony to the scoring along my back, but I could still toss a weak grin to Claudia as Crixus wound up to commence killing me.

Something in her face broke. It started with a subtle crack and burst forth in some unnamable emotion that shook her from crown to root. As the whip lanced agony along my spine, she broke through the ranks of spectators, running past Batiatus to grasp the post.

"Cantor, this isn't happening," she sobbed.

"Shhh," I soothed, throat raw and bleeding. "Dying's the easy part."

She clubbed me with a hand to the chest. It didn't hurt. I had worse to contend with.

"Come along, wench," snarled Batiatus, grabbing her arm. "Come away."

Claudia shrugged and Batiatus' hand flew away from her arm. "Back off!"

Back off?

"Listen, Cantor," her eyes drew close until they were the only things I could see, and her soft, slightly rough hands were the only thing I could feel as they cupped my face. A man could lose himself in that face. "This isn't real. None of this is."

"Now's not the time for religion, sweets."

"No, you idiot, it really isn't real. You aren't here. I'm not here. Here isn't here." The eyes disappeared and the next thing I knew her soft lips were at my ear. "Your name is Canton Alsate," she whispered. I felt an electric thrill across my skin and the pain of the whip faded a tad. "Apache warrior and agent for the BSI and you have been duped, pulled into a magical/tech simulation."

What the hell?

"Think *Matrix*, Canton," she continued. "It only works if you think it's real. Once you realize that none of this is real, then you can escape. This is a nightmare from which you can wake."

"What?" My back hurt, my wrists hurt from where they were shackled to the post and my brain seemed to be off-line.

"Escape!"

"Guards!" Batiatus sounded frantic, not a bit like himself at all.

"Hurry!"

Hurry. Right. *Matrix*?

So not unstuck in time. Not like Sam Beckett and all those other time travelers. No Morlocks or Elois or Odysseus or such. A trick, a ruse. But why?

Screw that with mayonnaise ... who cares why? What I needed was to get out. I opened my eyes to see the scene in a strange kind of slow motion as my mind started to race faster than the events unfolding around me.

"No," I said again, nice and loud. "No more."

The scene slowed, and I turned, the manacles no longer cuffing my wrists. The whip that Crixus used was uncurling toward me, filled with searing purpose and I said again, "No."

Crixus disappeared.

"No!" Batiatus disappeared.

"NO!" The *ludus*, the crowd ... they all disappeared leaving Claudia and I floating in a sort of grayish limbo.

"No," I whispered.

I disappeared.

CHAPTER NINE

Kal

———•———

Talk To Me

THERE IS NO SUCH thing as a blind Magician. Doesn't exist. Blind a Magician and you get a magic-less dude in need of a pair of concealing sunglasses. Apparently, they need sight to cast a spell, to help visualize the Shape of magic and where it would go.

Magic Using 101.

Twin licks of flame appeared, shiny and hot … right on the Magician's eyeballs. And I kept them there as he screamed his lungs out. Now, a normal flame would have been quickly doused by a pair of flapping hands, but this was magic fire so the only thing that happened when the Magician tried to snuff them out was to burn the heck out of his palms.

The forearm was gone from my throat … I could breathe again. Thank God. I took big gasping breaths as I kept an eye on the Magician who was screaming so loud they probably heard him in Hoboken.

My head felt like an overinflated balloon, ready to pop my eyeballs out and the pressure of holding the twinned spell brought bile to my throat.

One, two, three, four ... and stop.

The magic fires flickered out.

He kept screaming. Good. The more screaming, the less trying to kill me, that made me a happy camper.

Once again with the spell, this time on the zip tie around my right wrist. While Mr. Villain screamed, the nubbin of flame licked at the plastic, which began to burn slowly, dripping molten and flaming plastic down my forearm, although what I was going to do with the metal handcuff I didn't know, but first things first. The searing slowly traveled across my arm, had the hairs on the back of my head standing up and my teeth grinding against the burn, but I had to do something because when the fecal matter impacted upon the rotary oscillator, someone was going to try to make julienne fries out of mama Hakala's favorite son. Someone always tries.

Snap.

I released the spell as the first hint of Kal Flambé reached my nose and that's when things went from uncomfortably bad to seriously [DELETED] up.

Knock-knock. "Mr. H, you okay?"

Fantastic.

Of course, Mr. Villain, Mr. H, managed to a reply from where he was rolling around on the ground in excruciating pain. "No, you idiot! Help me!"

Flame still licked slightly along my forearm as the plastic continued to burn, but I'd been hurt a whole lot worse in my time on the job. In fact, having a trail of molten plastic drip down an arm handcuffed to headboard ranked somewhere around seventeenth or so, but there were more bad guys a-coming and that kicked my adrenal glands into high gear.

"Come on," I grunted, thrashing at the handcuff. No dice.

The doorknob rattled. Then the door nearly exploded as something massive slammed into it but held. Good craftsmanship.

Panic began to eat at the corners of my eyes, but I furiously ignored it and pulled. And pulled. My head throbbed. No go.

Thud! Thud!

That door wasn't going to hold out much longer. Blood burst from the skin under the handcuff as I pulled even harder, nearly dislocating my wrist, but I didn't stop, someone big was coming, Mr. H was screaming, and I needed out of there something fierce.

"Come on!" I screamed, giving one last pull on the cuff.

Something *popped* behind my eyes, a release of pressure like when you descend rapidly from a great height and suddenly I was filled with a staggering warmth that eclipsed every nerve ending, caused every hair on my body to perform a squat-thrust. Ginger spots appeared in front of my eyes and I tried to wipe them away, but my hands encountered nothing but my eyelids.

What?'

There they were, my hands ... with two shiny steel bracelets holding a couple links of broken chain. For a moment I wondered what happened, but another *thump* against the door, followed by an enormous *crunch* as it cracked from top to bottom, put some pep in my step and rocketed me onto my feet ...

...right onto the floor as a wave of fatigue slammed me upside the head. The world became a giant funhouse mirror where everything becomes wavy and loopy and your body either looks elongated like spaghetti or short and squat like a turnip and I was doing my best not to introduce my stomach contents to the bedroom floor. Like before in Omaha, I must have unconsciously cast a spell, but this time instead of a healing I was given enough strength to break my bonds, but the payoff was a wave of fatigue that ate at my mind like hamsters nibbling on a carrot.

BOOM! The door burst apart like rotten wood and what came through was human only in the sense that it looked like a man. Tall enough that it had to duck under the doorway and wide enough that it had to sidle in sideways, it was simply the most massive being I'd ever seen, and I'd seen ogres that looked like they could eat the entire Denver Broncos defensive line in one go.

Bulgy with muscles that moved like greased cables under dead black skin, the thing carefully eased through the doorway, which made me wonder how sturdy the door used to be considering it managed to withstand the Incredible Hulk for fifteen whole seconds. A red flannel shirt and blue jeans creaked alarmingly as they were stretched tight over the massive frame. "Mr. H?" it inquired in a curiously high-pitched, rather comical voice, like it had been huffing helium.

"Kill him!" screamed the agonized Magician still rolling on the floor.

Eyes like pools of frozen milk stared down at me. Yeech. "This one?"

"He's the only other one in here, you moron!"

"Okay." The thing started to raise an arm that could have doubled as a ship's mast. I had a brief vision of a *Looney Tunes* version of myself flat on the floor underneath a weight comically labelled '16 TONS'. Except there was no amount of re-inflating that could make me three-dimensional again.

What to do when you are about to be turned into strawberry jam, ground liberally into harvest gold cut-pile carpeting? Well, to be honest, there weren't any great options except one … at eye level.

With all my fading, fatigued strength I threw an enormous uppercut right to the big thing's giblets, using every erg of energy I had left, bringing the fist from the ground floor to the penthouse adding strength from ass and thighs.

Two-hundred plus pounds of angry Finn concentrated, distilled, down to four inches of knuckle impacting upon the thing's squishy nether regions. My fist buried itself deep into something softer than gonads and traveled upward a good foot before stopping. Those frozen milk eyes went wide and the thing let out a startled, high-pitched 'eep' before grasping at his tender bits and pitching over sideways to land on the thrashing Magician.

Fantastic.

I knelt there with my fist feeling tingly and gross from the soft, foam-like tissue of the creature who lay twitching and eeping and softly gasping while Mr. Villain lay there trying to catch his breath, barely able to wiggle under the enormous weight of whatever it was.

"Well, okay then." On my feet, swaying, but strength returning bit by bit. The rest of the house turned out to be three other empty rooms (including kitchen). Clean ...spotless, actually, eerily so. It looked like a house devoid of life, a sterile two-bedroom with ugly carpeting. I stumbled, realizing that my ankles were screaming, and I looked down, seeing the remnants of plastic zip-ties and handcuffs serving as bracelets. My feet were sheathed in the blood seeping from torn skin.

Back to the bedroom, a little more oomph in my step now. The thing on the Magician was still sleeping softly, eyes screwed shut and its plain, unremarkable, face closed like a door to all outside sensation.

One kick, then two, bruising my foot on the corner post, but it was enough to crack it loose. A few hard tugs later and I had a jagged club.

"Okay now," I said conversationally, puffing slightly. I felt ridiculous in my undies and nothing else, but a big stick helps with feelings of inadequacy. "My job is to do Supernaturals that wants to hurt people some dirty, so I hope you understand, whatever you are, that this isn't personal, is it? I mean, I'm a man of me word and I gave it to the Bureau to defend the colonies from beasties such as you."

I swung the club. The vibration from the impact on the thing's skull rendered my fingers numb for a moment. It felt like I hit a block of cement. Time for some elbow grease.

Thwack! The club splintered. Another hit and it split down the middle in a shower of toothpicks. My job was done, though, because the thing's skull lay misshapen and lumpy where I'd whacked it good and proper, a silvery fluid leaking out from where its tough flesh split.

"Good and done," I muttered, grabbing an enormous arm. Strong as I was, I felt like a four-year-old tugging on daddy's arm. A few minutes later I managed to roll the thing off of the Magician, who'd long since stopped his cursing and hollering. In fact, he looked a little blue and when the weight finally came off and he began to draw in great, big lungsful of air.

"Ah, good to know you're still amongst the land of the living, mate." I grabbed the Magician, who weakly scrabbled at my chest. He was a perfect fit for the bed, broken as it was.

Bouncy bouncy went the Magician on the mattress. He yelped. I grinned. What a good time. Now, I'm no sadist, mind you. Not the kind who gets his rocks off causing misery to others, but for a Magician who worked for a criminal organization that, at the very least, trafficked in children … well, let's just say I have some self-control issues.

Those issues manifested in Omaha when I tortured a bad guy. Sure, he had it coming, but I'm supposed to be one of the white hats, not the kind of bloke what blows kneecaps off just because I have my dander up. That earned me a ticket to a yearlong stint as Green Pea trainer and couch-sitter in a shrink's office. Not my concept of fun. Was it worth it? Maybe, but I'd been trying like hell to be a good guy ever since.

A few strips of bedsheet and Mr. Villain was bound at wrists and ankles, still screaming about his eyes, which looked like slightly burned egg whites.

"You bastard," he moaned. "You know what's going to [CENSORED] happen to you?"

"Ah, mate, the question you should be asking is what's going to happen to a certain blind magician." I stretched. "Now where are me clothes?"

"[CENSORED] you!"

"I'm really trying to maintain some composure here, you understand. I've been a wee off my feed ever since I met you organization arseholes in Omaha."

That got his attention. He turned his burned eyes toward

me and I shuddered at the slick, sick, bubbled whiteness. "What?" he asked.

"I was there, you know. I'm the bloke what found your little kiddie auction site and I shut it down hard, I did. Took some skin off me hide, not to mention removing the tongue of an angry Maori tribesman, but I managed. So, what you should be wondering is what the bloke who did such things, caused so much pain and shut down your little fun factory has in store for a freshly blind Magician who can't cast a spell to save his skin."

"Kal Hakala did all that."

"You got that right, mate."

A drop of sweat rolled off his forehead. "What? Are you saying—"

"That's right, boyo," I interrupted from a few short inches away. He flinched. "That's what I'm saying. What, you never heard of magic changing a bloke's looks and voice now? How's a fella to be all undercover-like if he so recognizable?" And that's when Mr. Villain began to shed some big, blubbery tears. I mean, he went to town on the whole face-crumpling-into-abject-terror thing. Really Oscar worthy, if you ask me. I guess I was the organization's version of the boogeyman.

"So sorry," he blubbered. "I didn't know."

"You wanted me here," I replied, no longer feeling anger or pity or much of anything. I was too worn out and so damn tired. That spellcasting took it out of me. "Now you got me, mate. First things first … me clothes."

"Closet. Please don't kill me."

Gosh, was my *reputation* that bad? I decided to roll with it. "Depends if you are going to cooperate or spend the last few moments of your life as a cheeky monkey."

"I'll cooperate," he cried. "Promise. Just get some help for my eyes!"

"No promises, mate. Those two look cooked well done, but I can always recommend leniency." The small sliding door closet held my clothes strewn all over the floor. My weapons were history. Probably in the van with Fake Tattoo and the rest of the party boys. Ah, my shoes. I needed those shoes. I loved those shoes. A smile crept up onto my face.

"Next." Damn, it felt good to be dressed and pressed. "Mr. Bad Guy Magician, please do yourself the great and good favor of telling me where you are keeping Canton Alsate." I crossed my arms, feeling a familiar dread creep into my guts. "And you better hope that he is still alive."

Mr. Villain was more than willing to talk. And talk. In fact, my ears began to feel a mite punished by the verbal diarrhea.

"Okay, okay, that's enough. Before I leave, I'd like a heads up on that thing that came through the door."

"What, the flesh golem?"

Uh-oh.

In the world of combating Supernaturals, even the most hard-bitten, ass-kicking, hard-hitting, head-taking genius agent (me, of course) can make a mistake. Believe me, I've made plenty in my long career and while usually the small ones only lead to scars, the big ones lead to being buried in a shoebox.

I'd just made a big mistake. I broke Hakala's Rule #1 When Fighting Monsters: Never Turn Your Back On A Supernatural Unless It's Been Rendered Into A Greasy Paste, And Not Even Then.

Golems are anthropomorphic beings created out of clay or stone using Jewish mysticism. The Hebrew word *emet*, or 'truth', is inscribed on the back of the head and, presto, an animated statue at your command. If one wanted to kill a golem, you had to blow it smithereens or remove the Hebrew letter *aleph* from the word *emet*, changing the meaning to 'death'.

What the mystics of the Dark Ages never learned was how to create a golem from human tissue. That was discovered by an Austrian surgeon/Magician Dr. Franzblau in the late 1600s, the genesis of the Frankenstein story. The advantages of the flesh golem over stone are that they can talk (because they started out with brains, even if they were abby-normal) and their ability to regenerate. In fact, you either had to disintegrate, or burn a flesh golem to ash to kill it.

See where I'm heading with this?

Airborne, not even registering the blow as such, more a sudden acceleration that had me zipping across the room at warp speed. The closet door slowed my horizontal traveling, powdering under my weight as I crashed on through into the closet where the sheetrock and studs were kind enough to conclude the deceleration trauma.

Splinters under me, splinters *in* me, my clothes a ruin, the skin underneath pretty much a loss as well. I slowly got to me feet amid a pile of kindling, just in time to barely dodge a fist the size of Montana, followed by an arm that could've doubled as a telephone pole.

"YOU HURT ME!" screamed the flesh golem, milky eyes wide in fury. His mouth looked like it was filled with flat, gray tombstones and its voice no longer seemed comical.

"YOU HURT ME!"

My left arm told me in no uncertain terms that it was no longer speaking to me except to say *ouch!* at every jostling movement and I was mortally afraid to look at the damage. The kind of fear you have when you think something monstrous and evil is breathing down your neck and you know if you turn around you'll find out exactly what's there and it won't be good, no ... not at all, so you keep your eyes forward in the hopes it will leave you alone and you can continue in peace. I knew that if I looked down I'd see a twisted, shattered mess that used to be my arm and I really, *really*, didn't want the reality of that thrust into my consciousness.

"YOU HURT ME!" screamed the golem. Apparently, he really resented my shot to his giblets. A giant fist grazed past my skull and I felt the sharp pain as the skin parted and blood began to flow.

How was I going to beat this flannel-covered nightmare before he turned me into Kal-flavored tomato paste?

Wait ... what? Oh ... flannel.

This was going to hurt.

Before that house-sized fist could draw back (I was stuck in a closet, it was a miracle I hadn't been flattened already) I envisioned the Zippo Spell Shape, calling it easily into mind and thrust outward toward that very flammable flannel. Then I did it again.

...and again.

...and again. And repeat. Twenty times in the span of a second-and-a-half. The front of the golem's flannel shirt erupted in flames and its wide, milky eyes, empty as a politician's soul, flew wide in shock. It began to flail around the room as the fire grew larger and larger until there was nothing more than a man-shaped pillar of fire whirling around the room emitting a high, fluting cry of pain and fear.

I gasped as the golem crashed full length onto the bed, smothering the Magician in fire, crushing him and the bed flat, flat, flatter than stale beer. Within seconds the room was filled with fire and smoke and my lungs began to burn, as if they'd been dipped and acid.

Hacking and coughing blood-flavored phlegm, I stumbled out the door as smoke chased me toward the front door. Outside I commenced to breathing air that wasn't trying to kill me.

A small, whitewashed, clapboard farmhouse in the middle of nowhere with the midday sun shining down in an almost cloudless sky. I took it all in for two whole seconds before the sudden realization that I was in agonizing pain forced me to look at the bones of my arm sticking out through my blood-soaked shirt.

Yep, as horrible as I thought it would be.

Gray/pink jagged shards stared back at me like an accusation, recrimination for not taking better care of myself and my knees buckled, my butt thumping hard on the driveway. All I could do was stare at my feet, my eyes shying away from the bloody bone sticking out through torn, red flesh and I wanted to cry, to scream, as the adrenalin rush that kept me going left me high and dry with the physical and emotional aftermath. The desire to wail and thrash and the shakes that took over my hands like a possession sent waves through me that I could barely contain. I knew it was the stress of everything I'd been through, all the hurt and the magic and my worry for Canton.

But it was more than that, too.

It was over a decade of putting my ass on the hot seat time and again and then getting up the next day in a repetitive pattern set forth by my initial desire to take vengeance against a Finnish demi-god. Now I had no excuse except to say I was addicted to the work, to the rush and the fear and the chase and, ultimately, the kill.

What did that say about me as a person?

No more excuses. I was a father, a husband and an agent and it was getting hard, so damn hard, to reconcile the three, to have them exist in the same universe. I knew deep down that something was going to give, like a dam bursting during hard rain and either my family or myself, probably both, was going to pay the price.

Fantastic.

During these maudlin thoughts, my mind flicked to my shoes. Unremarkable workaday, comfortable. The intel the Magician provided before he became a crispy critter came to mind and I grinned. Time for backup.

CHAPTER TEN

Canton

Welcome To The Real World

LIGHT, BRIGHT AND INTRUSIVE. Somewhat painful. Doggone annoying, actually.

"Gnnng … " The growl scraped past the sand in my throat. Small, hard hands cradled my head. "Easy there, Canton."

Canton. Me. Right, got it. My eyes opened and what I saw put my heart in a tailspin. Claudia. No, wait. Not Claudia, but Talya. No … hold that thought. Not Talya, This woman's face was older, harder, with crows feet around the eyes that hadn't deepened yet. It took a second because I'd left my brain back in Capua, but it hit me like a sledgehammer between the eyes.

"Omaha," I croaked around the sand. "You're that ninja lady who tried to exfoliate my skin down to the muscle."

Finely sculpted lips quirked. "You sound just like your friend, Hakala. Yeah, it's me." She grabbed my hands. Hers felt warm. "I know you have questions, but I'm not here to hurt you."

Damn but she had some brown eyes. Soft, deep and virtually magical. Talya's eyes … Claudia's eyes. They almost made me believe her. "Why do I feel so weak?"

"You've been here for two weeks."

"What?"

"Two weeks."

"Is that why I feel I can't even get out of my own way?"

"That's it. You've been hooked into the Loop for two weeks, fed intravenously and kept as comfortable as possible."

The Loop. Caught her use of the capital. I thought back to my experiences in Capua and Troy and realized that somebody actually went and done created the real-world version of *The Matrix*. But it felt so real, the hard, hot crack of the whip against my back, the feel of Aeneas' skin as I beat the crap out of him. So real, the memories vivid as the glare of the noonday sun.

While my head felt has heavy as an anvil, I still tried to lever it up off what turned out to be a comfy down pillow. My stomach muscles protested, and my spine popped and cracked just like my grandfather, Nantan Lupan's, used to after a nap. No matter how much I wished it to be otherwise, the years were creeping up on me. Time always wins.

With a little help from the assassin lady, I managed to get to my feet. I was set up in one of those embarrassing blue hospital gowns where your bare ass hangs out the back and you know everyone's looking. A chill slid along my crack and I maneuvered one hand to close the gown in back. The assassin lady smiled knowingly.

Two spare cots in a small steel shed. IV rack, heart monitor, an EEG, and a strange looking little loop of dark plastic attached to a small black box. A tiny AC unit chugged in the corner. It looked like a low-rent Frankenstein's lab. The other cot also had its fair share of medical equipment along with one of those loop things.

A body lay on the floor, a guy in black lying next to an M4. His throat looked lumpy and distorted and I tossed a look to the assassin lady, noticing that she wore plain old jeans and a Metallica t-shirt.

I examined the dead guy critically. In good shape, but

smaller than the average man, about five-foot-three, so too small for me to loot the body for his tactical gear, which sucked because that meant my crack would have to hang out for a little while longer.

"He would've stopped me from waking you. The organization that hired me isn't long on trust ... for good reason."

The organization. Those dildos who trafficked in kids, a chock-full-o-nuts group of bad guys in need of killing. A lot. This did not inspire a whole lot of trust for a lady who killed at their request. I felt an anxious tingle along my spine. Why did she wake me? What was her end game? I needed a weapon.

"You still working for them?"

"That body is my letter of resignation."

Quite a letter, one nobody could get wrong. I examined the dead guy. Pretty good shape, a mercenary if I had a guess. Buzz cut, wide shoulders and a sneer on his lips that persisted in death, a doggone sure sign that he'd been an asshole of epic proportions in life. I separated myself from the ninja assassin chick and picked up the M4. Cold and heavy. Good.

"What do I call you?" The sand was leaving my throat and a couple of coughs cleared it away.

"Pardon?"

"Can't call you Ninja Assassin Chick. Sounds sexist." I checked the mag. Full. The weapon had been well maintained. I lifted the M4, not quite pointing it at her. Those slightly almond eyes grew round. "Now, I don't want to seem ungrateful, but you've got some 'splaining to do."

"What do you plan on doing, Agent Alsate?" she asked.

"I plan on listening to you reddening my ears with a story about how all this came about."

"Beginning where?"

"At the beginning ... with you. Then when I entered that diner in town, you know the one. After that, things get kinda hazy."

"So. Everything."

"Everything."

"Do we have time for this?" she asked.

I chuckled with more mirth than I felt. "We're in no rush. Unless there's a bunch of bad guys waiting outside this shed door?"

"No. Just you and me for a little bit. I checked." The assassin stretched, long and slow and I couldn't help but watch. For a slender little lady, she packed a wallop. "Do you mind if I smoke?" she asked.

"Bad habit but go ahead."

"Most are. In my line of business, it's not the smoking that kills you."

I shrugged. "Fair enough. Go ahead."

The assassin produced a pack of menthols from a back pocket and lit it with a BIC that had seen better days. She drew the smoke in deep, savoring it as if it would be her last one. Perhaps it would. I wasn't in what you would call a very forgiving mood, but she did pull me out of the Loop, so I was willing to cut her some slack. For now.

She sat on the couch while I stood there somewhat unsteadily on the cold steel floor, ass hanging out of my hospital gown and feeling stretched and worn to a nubbin. The ninja assassin chick sat down on the couch and began to speak in dull monotone.

***

So, YOU WANT TO KNOW what happened and why it happened? Easy enough, Agent Alsate, easy enough.

My name is Barbara Kahale. That's something no one knows because I buried it long time ago. It can't be found on any database. A lot of money went into deleting and destroying every last shred of my past, so you should see this as a kind of trust-building exercise, Canton, and proof of my sincerity. All that is for another day, that is if I have any more.

Long story short, I'm an assassin. Pay me enough money and I'll kill. One rule though, no children, no innocents. That may sound strange, but there are enough bad people in the world no need to be taking out the good ones. The people I kill usually have resumes that would make Satan blush. That's not an excuse, merely an explanation of how things are.

The entity you call the organization hired me a couple of years ago to terminate a woman who was involved in white slavery, the kidnap and selling of women to rich Middle Eastern types for their harems. Personal sex slaves.

This woman was shorting the organization on their cut of the profits, something they didn't take kindly to. Their Magicians are mostly a cowardly bunch, not willing to take risks, so they hired outside help. I disappeared the woman, gave the police an anonymous tip about her operation (I maybe a killer, but I'm no monster) and faded into the night. After that the organization used my services more and more. After a while, they trusted me enough to attempt recruitment, informing me about the World Under and magic and Supernaturals and all the scary things in and out of this world.

I refused.

They still used my services because I offered results and, truthfully, who was I going to tell? The whole Supernatural thing didn't come out until last year. Soon after the Omaha fiasco.

That's where we met, of course. Where you used magic to keep me from shooting you and then proceeded to beat me like a rug. I've never met anyone as fast as you, as graceful in combat. And here I thought I was the dangerous one.

I know, I know, hold your horses. This is merely plot exposition so I can get to the heart of the story, the meat and bones of how you were put into the imaginary world.

CHAPTER ELEVEN

Barbara

———•———

Bait

THE PARK BENCH ALMOST burned my butt when I sat. It was noon and the sun was brutal overhead and I was feeling a little cranky. The email sent to my Outlook account implied that the organization had a job for me and to reply with utmost haste. I responded by saying I'd meet them in the park.

Why the park? Have you seen how busy it is at noon? Place is packed to the rafters with joggers and people on their lunch hour. Sometimes it feels as if the entire population of New York City is crammed in there. You can get lost in a sea of humanity and it's a perfect place to fade away in case a job heads south.

"On time. Punctual as ever, Ms. Versa."

My contact with the organization sat next to me. Called himself Mr. G. Dressed like the typical mid-level office drone in a short-sleeved button-down shirt with a pocket protector holding three gel pens and sporting a black string tie. Soft around the middle, short black hair and the dead eyes of a landed carp. You looked at him, maybe noticed him for the drone he was, then promptly forgot all about him the second you looked away. Urban camouflage … dress the predator up as a house pet and the rank and file of humanity never notices. It's how the organization stayed under the radar for so long.

As for me, I made do with business lady chic and blended in quite nicely myself. "Can you even afford me?" I asked. "You people have been hunted to the ends of the earth, scoured root and branch. How much money do you have left?"

Mr. G pursed his lips primly and opened a scuffed, brown leather briefcase. Inside was a sandwich and a juice box. He bit into a PB&J and chewed for a bit before answering. "Plenty enough to hire you."

"Good. What's the job this time?"

He turned his dead eyes toward me. "How would you like to get even with the agent who beat you in Omaha, Ms. Versa?"

A tingle ran across my cheeks, but I kept my face expressionless. "Canton Alsate." According to all the television shows, Canton Alsate was Kal Hakala's best friend and the only other agent in the Bureau who could stand toe-to-toe with him in a fight. Perhaps he was even a little better than Hakala. Sure bested me quick and dirty. Professional pride warred with the fear in my heart. The image of Alsate's blurring hands and deep brown eyes caused an unusual flutter in my stomach that must've been fear.

"Yes. The Apache himself."

"You want me to kill the man who kicked my ass?"

"Don't you want a second shot at him?"

It wasn't about second shots. My daddy may've been a complete idiot and total bastard, but he actually left me one bit of sound advice between all the whippings: 'always choose your battles, never fight one you can't win'. Shows that even complete assholes can have a few active brain cells. "I'm not in the business of revenge. Keeps me alive."

"You're in luck then. We don't want you to kill him, merely incapacitate him for a while. What you do after that, when he's at your mercy, is up to you. We will be offering support in this matter."

"Should I decide to take the contract."

"Yes."

"I work alone," I said. "Keeps the idiots out of the equation."

Mr. G frowned. It was not attractive. "We have hired the best private contractors and will be supplying you with a Magician as well. One of our most capable, a Mr. H."

Well, that was a horse of a different color. A Magician meant that the organization had a hard-on and was looking to cause some major damage. This elevated the situation from the normal 'take out the bad guy who can't play nice with bosses' to a serious scorched earth policy. "This alphabet nomenclature is wearing on me, G." The citizens of New York passed by, each encased in a universe that didn't include the others. "Tell me what's going on."

"None of your business," he replied primly, a small dot of grape jelly at the corner of his mouth like a tiny, purple jewel. "Do you want the contract or not?"

My nose was telling me that something didn't smell right here. "Okay. No. Have a nice day." I stood.

"Wait!"

I sat, staring a hole in Mr. G.

"All right, dammit," he seethed. "You win. We need you and your skills."

"Double the rate."

"Done."

I blinked. Another gig like this and I could retire. That sounded pretty good to me. "Spill."

"We want to use you as bait to lure Alsate to a location of our choosing in an effort to garner valuable intel and to trap Hakala. The heads of the organization want him, and they want him yesterday. They feel that the timing is right."

"Timing?"

"Hakala has been training recruits for about a year and our sources tell us he's about to quit or be reinstated as a field agent."

Everyone knew, thanks to all the talk shows and the various

cable news networks, that Hakala was training what he called Green Peas to be the next agents in the Bureau, but no one would have that kind of intelligence on the man unless …

"You have someone inside!" I blurted.

His grin was pure smugness.

That was another off-colored equine. The fact that the organization had a mole in the most paranoid, disciplined, *dangerous* law enforcement in US history was an achievement of staggering proportions. I held back from the obvious questions because I knew he wasn't about to answer, instead I asked, "Seems like a lot of resources for revenge. Why?"

"Not revenge," he answered. "Well, not entirely. Mostly it has to do with information." Another bite of the PB&J. "There is an emergency response at the Bureau called Fortress of Solitude. It's the failsafe in event of catastrophic collapse of its defensive systems. We're not sure what it does, but our intel suggests that when the FOS protocol is enacted, Warehouse is rendered unassailable by ordinary means, even extraordinary ones like a nuclear strike. Senior agents have the activation and deactivation codes for the FOS protocol. We want those codes."

"So Alsate."

"Yes."

"Or Hakala."

He nodded. "Exactly."

It took a minute. "You plan on taking down the Bureau."

No reply to that epiphany.

"You realize that you could wind up killing innocent people," I whispered.

Mr. G smiled thinly. "No one there is innocent. Let's just say that this will help re-establish our American operations." He drank from the juice box straw until it made a hollow, slurping sound. "Now you know. Trepidations?"

Several, actually. "None."

"Good. Head to Birmingham, Alabama immediately. You will be met at the airport by our people. This is non-negotiable, by the way. You will be transported to the town of Talladega where you will eventually be noticed by the Bureau's AI after you visit an ATM to withdraw some small amount of funds from a dummy account we've set up."

"AI? The Bureau has AI?"

"A singular entity not mentioned in the press briefings or depicted in that deplorable movie about that Denver mission. It's the Bureau's ace in the hole, so to speak."

A damn big ace, if you asked me. No wonder they're Johnny on the spot. This was beginning to smell worse and worse, but since my conditions had been met, I could hardly go back on my word. I merely nodded, and he stood, dusting crumbs from his cheap black slacks.

"Good doing business with you. Ms. Versa."

***

LET ME TELL YOU, THOSE mercs the organization hired were real bottom of the barrel boys. I mean they were thick as a brick and not as quick, more muscle than sense, more guns than knowhow. They could fight, of course, but not that well. Proof that the organization was trying to pinch a penny until Lincoln screamed. Probably spent most of their roll on my contract.

"You think he's comin'?"

That was Drake, the head merc. Not as stupid as the others, but definitely not the sharpest knife in the drawer. Tall, buff and deft enough with a pistol, but I wasn't about to turn my back on him ... there was something wrong with his eyes, something broken, like gemstones with large cracks running crazy through them.

Nina's was crowded with the usual suspects, locals who loved the food and the random out-of-towners who were directed there by said locals. I toyed with my tri-tip and garlic mash, taking sips of the glass of incredibly sweet tea that threatened to turn me diabetic. "Of course, he'll come," I said absently.

"Can't wait. Always wanted to tangle with one of them Bureau types."

My sudden bark of laughter startled the other patrons, but they looked away when I covered my mouth with a hand. The mercs had yet to put the fear of God into the locals, but they would and all it would take was a couple of weeks and a mysteriously dead sheriff, something I didn't approve of or condone. "Do you have a death wish?" I sneered behind my fingers. "Any one of them could turn you into a pretzel in two seconds."

Drake snorted and flexed impressive muscles. "Listen—"

"Hssst!" I hssst-ed. One thing I can say about Drake, he knew how to take orders. He cut the chatter and I indicated with the roll of the eyes the man who just walked through the door.

Of course Canton Alsate was a pretty popular guy, being Hakala's best friend and one of the best agents to ever serve his country, but the guy who walked in the door would've been overlooked by most people because of the disguise he wore: ruddy skin leached of color until the tone looked like a light spray tan instead of Native American red. Black hair cut short and curly and streaked with auburn accompanied by a similarly colored handlebar moustache under brown eyes rendered gray with scleral contact lenses. Slap his lean, muscular frame into a pair of Duluth Firehose slacks and green t-shirt that read KISS MY @$$ and you had a guy that most people wouldn't recognize as the second most popular agent for the Bureau.

I ain't most people. How could I forget those shoulders? Those wide hands and, for God's sakes, those *cheekbones*? I could shave my legs with those things! If he wasn't so damn sexy I wouldn't have remembered him from Adam.

I adjusted my blonde wig, the only attempt at a disguise. Wasn't trying to fool him anyway. Alsate sat at table for two and waited for a server.

"You know what to do," I whispered as I stood. "Don't blow this."

A sullen "I won't" followed me as I sauntered away.

The trick wasn't to fool Alsate. The trick was to make him *think* I was trying to fool him, so I went with the amateur move of a blonde wig letting him think that I thought it was enough to fool the average joe. He wasn't the average joe.

I kept my eyes away from the Apache, staring straight ahead as I walked past. It took him less than a second for the pattern of my face to register in his brain and he stood so fast I thought I could hear his body whistle through the air. Before his hand could grasp my arm, I slid nimbly away, avoiding him as if by accident.

"You! Stop!"

Why do people think that by yelling stop the person you want stopped will comply? I mean, come on! Oh well, I guess we all do it, sort of a gut reaction. Of course, I didn't stop, I kept putting my back to him while heading toward the door.

"Hey mister, leave the girl alone."

Girl? Was Drake being deliberately insulting? I made sure to not let the door hit me on the ass as I exited, and what happened next, I saw through the plate glass windows that fronted the diner.

I almost missed it.

Drake grabbed Alsate by the wrist before the other man could bolt after me, his muscles bulging as he applied pressure to fragile bones. Alsate seemed to blur and then Drake found himself flying through the air as if he had a missile jammed up his ass. Alsate stood there, wig askew and glowering before dashing the hairpiece off and heading toward the door.

I beat feet, sure that Alsate would follow.

In an alley a block away I turned and waited, chest aching not from exertion, but from anticipation. Did I want this to happen? To lure Alsate into the clutches of the organization and possible death? To be perfectly honest ... not really. I admired the man despite the beating I took from him in Omaha and didn't want to see him captured by the worst people on the planet, people that would make an African warlord shriek in terror.

But I gave my word and, in my business, that's the most important thing in the world. Without it, I have no business and most likely would be decorating the bottom of a grave somewhere.

Alsate sped around the corner of the alley in hot pursuit, weapon in hand … a sleek looking Colt. He stopped abruptly, no doubt smelling the trap that was there.

"It's you," he said flatly, eyes darting everywhere.

"Leave me alone," I growled, raising my fists. "Just leave right now."

A cautious step or two closer and eyes that seemed to focus on everything around. This guy wouldn't go easy. "You know I can't do that." He didn't quite point the gun at me.

Perhaps he saw something in my eyes, or the faint whisper of cloth against cloth, or even smelled the musky tang of men's aftershave. Whatever it was, one sec he was standing just inside the alley, the next he was a blur across concrete as the twin prongs of a Taser flashed past his shoulder trailing lines of copper wire.

Nine men rushed the alley, all the mercs assigned to the case, the best the organization could get on the down low. All had Tasers and cattle prods and were dressed in the best tactical gear money can buy. The plan was to overwhelm and take Alsate alive. No plan survives first contact with the enemy.

Canton Alsate spun, firing two shots. Two mercs fell lifeless as each took a bullet to the face, almost comical looks of surprise on their faces. A moment later the gun hit the alley floor as a cattle prod knocked it out of the Apache's hand, but a Bowie knife that could've doubled as a short sword suddenly appeared there as if by magic.

Then he got to work.

Spinning to the side, he delivered a vicious slash to a merc's arm, opening it to the bone while kicking another solidly in the crotch. That merc folded up and decided to sit this fracas out. Drake appeared around the corner and tried for a Superman punch, launching himself into the air with his arm cocked back, ready to deliver a blow with his entire weight behind it. Alsate saw it coming and delivered a devastating spin kick that bounced Drake off the alley wall before he could land.

That big knife flashed, cleaving flesh as easily as it did the air and two more mercs went down screaming, holding in great purple loops of intestine and the rest of the mercs, perhaps realizing that going after the agent one by one was a tactical mistake, charged. Within a second the Apache was buried under a mound of mercenary idiots who began to kick and punch and hammer at him with their cattle prods.

"Oh, you morons," I muttered. "Why am I always stuck with the idiots?" A scream interrupted my disgust. And another.

The pile of mercs practically flew apart, propelled by an enraged Apache. It looked like that knife was going to be inserted into some places that weren't meant to have things inserted into them when Alsate finally caught a pair of Taser prongs in the left shoulder.

"[DELETE]ing Indian," growled one of the mercs as the Apache jittered and juked before falling to the ground in a twitching heap. The idiot pulled a revolver and pointed it at the helpless agent, finger tightening on the trigger.

"No!" yelled Drake, still sending current to his victim.

Fear coursed through me, galvanizing me into action. My fist connected to the merc's jaw, spraying teeth across the alley and dropping him like a side of beef next to Alsate.

"Idiot," I growled, delivering a kick to the downed merc, putting his lights out. "I would so like to work with professionals one day."

CHAPTER TWELVE

Canton

What Now?

Barbara's words trickled away like sand from between my fingers and I stood there watching her impassively, my mind whirling and jinking a thousand miles an hour as I took it all in. Somehow the organization had known about the nanolocator in my butt cheek and either removed or neutralized it. Either way it explained why Kal hadn't ridden in like a white knight and killed every last one of the creeps who held me. I tried to remember the fight, finding Barbara in the diner … everything, but it was clean out of my skull, erased by trauma or magic or perhaps an aftereffect of the Loop.

None of that really pressed at me because there was one question that topped the rest. "Why were you in the Loop?" I asked.

She lit another cigarette. "To open you up. To have you fall in love with me, to be the damsel in distress you'd latch onto. Your profile suggests you have a fierce protective instinct, and if we could exploit that we could get you to open up fully, open your *mind* with your cooperation. Then we'd have the FOS code that we couldn't retrieve otherwise by magic."

"Surrender to you in the Loop would surrender my mind?"

A shake of the head. "No, it merely allows access so we could ransack your brain for a specific piece of data."

Bile splashed the back of my throat as my finger tightened on the trigger. She caught the motion. Not much got past her, it seemed. "And then?"

"The mercy of a bullet."

"What about the team shadowing me? I had backup."

"I don't know. You were my primary, the only one I was contracted to deal with. At best guess, Drake and the others ambushed your fellow teammates and buried them in shallow graves. My guess is that they disabled their nanolocators as well."

Rage hit me hard and I nearly did it ... nearly completed the pull to spatter her brains all over the shed, but that's not how I was raised. Nantan Lupan would not have approved. "Why did you help me?" The team. More good people lost to the grinder. I wanted to cry but held it back. There was work to be done.

Those dark, dark eyes found mine. "Because the plan worked, but in reverse."

Reverse?

Oh my. "Are you saying—?"

"I fell for you in there," she said hollowly, deflating slightly until she seemed a pile of raw nerves.

Ten kinds of emotion warred within me and I nearly dropped the M4. "What?" I said through numb lips.

"You heard me."

Yeah, I did. I sat on the cot next to her. "I can't hardly believe it."

Barbara drew her legs up and held them in the circle of her arms, resting her cheek on her knees. "There's nothing more surprising to me to find out that the man of my dreams belongs to the agency that wants to put me down."

What a doggone fix this was. I shook my head and took my finger off the trigger. "What now?"

I felt her eyes on my skin. "What what now?"

"About getting out of here. What do I have to look for?"

"A couple of techs and four other asshat mercenary types with more muscles than brains. The usual morons, you know the type."

Man, oh man, did I ever. My eyes flicked to the merc lying all dead like and realized that this incredibly beautiful, incredibly *dangerous*, woman had just permanently severed ties with the organization in the most dramatic way possible. Her life was forfeit if they ever caught wind of her.

"Where are they?"

"Techs are eating lunch in the house with the mercs," she replied through a drift of cigarette smoke. "After that, it's wide open. Way I figure it with the full weight of law enforcement around the globe pressing in, the organization can't mount large offensives anymore. We take care of those six people and we're home free."

"We?"

A small smile. "A girl can hope."

I was still madder than a wet hen at Barbara, but she did get me out of a sticky situation. The chances I might have surrendered to a mind rape were pretty high and toward the end of that whipping I was losing my ability to say no. At what point did my duty to the Bureau outweigh an obligation to the person who saved my life? Not to mention the doggone lives of those had I given up the FOS protocols.

She did lure me down there in the first place, though. *Arrrghh!* It was enough to drive a body mad.

I stood. "You stay here, I'm gonna take care of some business at the house."

Barbara stood as well. "I'm coming with."

"No."

There'd been enough women in my life that when she crossed her arms and gave me a good, steely glare, I knew she was setting in for some epic arguing. "Look at you, you can barely stand. It's been two weeks of relative inactivity and your muscles are likely to cramp up when you go into combat, not to mention that you don't know the layout of the house, how far away it is, or what the mercs are armed with. You. Need. Me."

I hate it when I'm at the wrong end of an argument. "To hell with this," I groused. "I'm outtie."

And I was. Straight out the shed with Barbara at my heels and it took all I had to stumble my way out into the sunshine. My knees almost buckled, but I wasn't about to let her see me falter.

From behind. "Easy there, Tex."

Doggone it.

A two-story whitewashed house stood at the other side of a huge, well-kept lawn that looked like it could've graced the back nine at Pebble Beach. As my eyes adjusted, I realized how very far away the building was and how racked and packed I felt.

"You okay, Cowboy?"

"Fine. And I'm an Indian, not a cowboy."

"Really? Semantics before combat?"

"Shut up."

This witty repartee might have gone on for a bit longer, but as we reached the back porch, the door opened, and two people came out carrying a couple of cans of A&W.

On the left, a thin guy in a lab coat, on the right a woman dressed the same, but with sensible shoes instead of sneakers and both of them wore identical expressions of shock. I cleared the three steps to the porch and gave the dude a hard uppercut that laid him back and down through the door where he landed with a resounding crash. So much for being weak after two weeks in the Loop.

Doggone it, I thought as I stared up at the ceiling from where I lay on the porch, legs gone all wet noodle and shoulders feeling like I just pushed a tractor uphill. The world did a little wiggle-wobble and spots moved into my field of vision as the lady tech (had to be the techs, right? The mercs would never wear lab coats) started with some good old down-home screaming, which cut off abruptly as Barbara flew into my field of vision. There came a couple of *thuds* and a *crunch*, followed by a *thump* and all was still.

"Help me up, wouldya?" I groaned as I tried to coax some life into my limbs.

"What? A big, strapping agent like you doesn't need help from a little girl like me."

"Oh, shut up."

Laughter and a pair of surprisingly strong arms lifted me to my feet sparking a wave of dizziness that passed in a moment.

"Love your hospital gown. Your butt looks so adorable."

Yes, a Native American can turn even brighter red. "Shut up." And, because I didn't want to seem ungrateful. "Thanks for taking care of the other one."

"Be still my beating heart."

She might have fallen for me and been all apologetic-like, but she still managed to give me grief as if she was actually my girlfriend, and I couldn't decide if that was a good or bad thing.

"Come on," I grumped quietly as we entered the house. "Let's find those mercs before they find—"

I dove to the right as bullets ripped through the spot my skull used to occupy and I hit the ground rolling, colliding into a coffee table that didn't do my shoulder any good. Hard pain paralyzed my left arm as furniture collapsed under me in a heap of splinters.

Before I could gather my wits, an Uzi-toting moron appeared out of a doorway to my left and raised the weapon. I felt my stomach clench in fear just before the barrel of that weapon met my eyes and I mentally began my last prayer.

A flash of silver followed by a resounding *thunk* and the merc, dressed in really nifty black tactical gear, disappeared back through the door, leaving the Uzi to land on old shag carpeting. I could hear the thud his body made as he landed. and I let loose a soft chuckle of relief.

Barbara helped me up and handed me the M4. "Try not to drop it next time, Canton."

Things weren't really going my way, were they? "What happened to him?"

She smiled. "Ashtray." She took hold of the Uzi and aimed through the doorway. I placed a hand on the weapon.

"Alive. The Bureau will want to question him."

Before she could object, bullets rained down from the ceiling and one traced a line of fire down my shoulder blade. I hissed and dove toward a floral love seat while Barbara made use of an old table in the dining area.

Fingers and hands flew as plaster drifted down. "I think they know we're here," she signed in American Sign Language, or Amslan. Go figure that she did enough background on me to know I volunteered at the Cleary School for the Deaf on Long Island during my junior and senior years in high school. Colleges love that kind of thing.

The language came back to me quickly, even though it had been years since I last made use of signing. "You think?"

"Three more."

"We can't charge up the stairs, they'll cut us to pieces."

"Well then, smart guy, what next?"

I grinned. "You got a smoke?"

***

"DID ANYONE TELL YOU YOU'RE a complete bastard?" Not an insult.

I let out an evil smile. Kal would have been proud of my ingenuity. "Been around the best, you know." The techs lay on the ground at our feet, along with the Uzi toting merc, naked as a jaybird and still in a blissful state of not bothering us at all. I'd stripped him of his black tactical gear because I didn't want to be flashing my crack for all the world to see, but the outfit was made for someone three inches shorter and narrower in the hips. A bit tight in the crotch.

Our weapons were trained on the house, the bottom floor belching fire and smoke into the air. When I asked for a smoke, what I really wanted was a cigarette lighter. One way to flush out the guys upstairs, although a little hard on the property value.

A dormer window exploded outward, letting loose a billowing cloud of black smoke and a black clad body flew through the air, arcing toward the ground near where we stood half-hidden in the shade of an empress maple.

The merc landed beautifully in a tuck and roll (a perfect 10 if this was the Jumping-Out-The-Window event at the Summer Olympics) bounding to his feet, Mac-10 ready to spray a shower of bullets as the glass thudded into turf. Before his finger could tighten on the trigger, the butt of the M4 hit him straight on the nose, smearing it across his cheeks and dropping him like a steer in a slaughterhouse.

Beside me the Uzi coughed, and someone screamed from the dormer window. "Had to do it," Barbara said. "She was going to shoot you."

Doggone it ... male prejudice tweaked me as I felt a momentary shudder of remorse for that woman in the house. Even women can be asshat mercs, although Nantan Lupan would not have approved.

"...*cough* ... throwing my weapon ... *cough cough* ... out!" This from inside the house. A second later an AR16 hit the lawn.

"Don't really feel like killing anyone," I yelled. "So, come on out, but if you try anything, you'll die."

The last merc leapt out and failed to score in the Jumping-Out-The-Window event as he landed awkwardly, and something gave with a wet *snap*. A lot of screaming after that, a hell of a lot.

"Should we help him?" I asked.

Barbara snorted. "I don't think I'm medically qualified."

I stared at the merc, wondering if I should render aid, but was interrupted by a deep-throated rumble that came from the front of the house and I ran around, jumping the split-rail that surrounded the back yard, the effort staggering me a bit ... still not fully recovered from my enforced vacation in the Loop.

Coming down a long gravel driveway was a Harley Fatboy throwing out a plume of dust that nearly obscured the Nissan Armada following. I raised my weapon, eye traveling down the sight line to the biker's skull as he blazed toward me at a blinding clip. Something about that big guy, the set of his shoulders, set some bells ringing in my ears, but I didn't let myself become distracted.

There was no way I was going to be taken again. The organization would have to tear the FOS codes from my bleeding corpse before I'd go down again.

"Get ready, Barbara."

No answer.

Doggone it.

I placed gentle pressure on the trigger ... the biker was mine, dead bang. A few more feet and he'd see me clear and swerve, so it was now or never.

As if reading my mind, the biker slewed to a stop, leaping off the motorcycle, letting it fall to the ground and the Armada braked hard. The biker began a long walk toward me through a cloud of dust, slowly raising his hands to grasp his helmet. Six people exited the Armada, rolling out with weapons drawn, pointed toward the ground.

"Canton?" yelled the biker.

"That's close enough," I replied when he came within thirty feet. "No farther."

The helmet fell to ground revealing a bearded face. "Not late for the dramatic rescue, am I?" he said in a thick, British accent.

"Who are you mister?"

"Don't be shooting an old friend, mate, or Jeanie would have ya ta task, she will."

As if summoned, Jeanie slunk her long form out of the Armada. I sighed, lowering the weapon and nearly fainted as she planted a kiss on the stranger's lips.

Why would—oh, yeah ... magic, right? "Kal?"

"Wot? You never seen a Finn in disguise, have you?"

CHAPTER THIRTEEN

Kal

———◆———

End of Daze

"AGENT HAKALA, AGENT ALSATE." If Andrea was surprised at the two most senior agents showing up out of the blue, she sure didn't show it. "I'm afraid Director Bauer isn't in; he's taken some private time."

That alone would've set most people's hair on fire, the thought of BB taking time off. It just didn't fit. Kind of like an elevator in an outhouse.

"Understood." I grinned and placed my hands on the desk, so the spell Shapes could read my aura and whatnot so as not to obliterate my tender bod. "Picking up some paperwork for the transition."

"And I'm along for the ride." Canton placed his hands down once I was finished.

Andrea's right hand emerged from under the desk ... from the butt of a shotgun or some technomagic doodad that would render us into slurry, I wasn't sure. Finally, she showed some emotion. I think it was ... amusement? Not sure. Kind of like watching a glacier grin.

I turned to go, then suddenly turned back. Andrea didn't

startle. Nerves of steel. "When I'm done, I'll need you to come in. We need to talk about the role of the Receptionists." Actually, we never called them that anymore because they were now the public faces of the Bureau, the publicists, spin doctors, PR, whatever, but I was old fashioned. I heard that the new moniker stuck to them was, quite simply, The Flacks.

"Why?" Now there was puzzlement. That was number two. Time to go for the trifecta.

"Because I want you looking at me and not Canton."

She almost made it. Almost. Just as her body swiveled in her chair, fist suddenly filled with six inches of gleaming steel, Canton smacked her on the back of the neck with a spell gem. She slumped.

Lights out.

***

"So why did Andrea betray the Bureau?"

I leaned back in the Director's chair and felt its ripe plushness envelop my backside. Oh yeah, I could get used to that. "The organization has her family. Father, mother and younger brother," I said from my seat of Ultimate Comfort. "Comply or they die ... pretty much the organization's motto."

My wife made a face. "She should have come to us."

"The organization performed a complete psych profile on people working in the Bureau, easy enough to do now that everything is out in the open. They found out that Andrea's only weakness, her only fear, is of losing her family. They played her well, offering up proof of life via a burner smartphone. In her mind, she had no other choice. Not that I'm condoning her actions. Right now, all the alphabet agencies are searching for her family and we have a couple of magicians who are aces with divination in on it, too."

Jeanie and I enjoyed some precious alone time in the enormous office that BB vacated. No one knew where he went, only that he was taking his accrued vacation time. Turned out to be about six months' worth. I'd just returned from Andrea's interrogation and processing, it was now up to the DOJ to decide what to charge her with and to pass sentence. It was up to me not to think about it anymore.

Fanfreakingtastic.

Still, good to be back and no longer bespelled, no longer sounding like a character from a Guy Ritchie movie, thank goodness, but there came a price with all the new responsibility and I felt a sneaking suspicion that it would be a lack of sleep. Uneasy rests the head that wears the Boss Hat, or some such.

"How did you get in touch with the Bureau stuck out in the middle of nowhere without a mobile?" Jeanie asked. "You never told me."

"Shoe phone."

Jaw dropped. It was wonderful to behold. "*What?*"

"A. Shoe. Phone." I said slowly. "A phone in my shoe."

"Like in that silly old spy series on the telly, *Get Smart*?"

"Yeah, but much cooler, and smaller. Had Alex install it for me. Thought it might come in handy."

Jeanie face-palmed. "I married a great, big, ruddy idiot."

"Not to mention handsome and resourceful. Oh, and humble."

A groan. I tried not to smile.

All looked to be right with the world. Canton got out alive even though the ninja assassin chick disappeared when I showed up with the cavalry.

Speak of the devil, the door at the far end of the office opened and my best bud strolled through like he owned the place.

"Hey, white boy."

"Hey, Canton." I gestured toward the wet bar. "Want a snort."

He shook his head and gave Jeanie a peck on the cheek. "Looking good, Hot Stuff."

"Well, aren't you a charmer," she replied, standing. "I'll

leave you two testosterone filled heavyweights alone for some boy time. Don't stay out too late."

"And so, it begins," I muttered as she sashayed away. What a fine sight that sashay was, indeed.

"So, you're the big guy." My friend sounded unimpressed.

"That's what it says on the front of my underwear."

"Gahh!" Canton through up his hands. "That hurt."

My smile reached my ears. "Maybe someday you will be a master at snark, grasshopper."

"Oh, lord help me and pass the wine."

We sat there in comfortable silence, two old friends taking our ease in a strange, new world and sea change of status. I was now his superior and that was an unfamiliar road for me and I wasn't certain it would be the right fit, it might chafe now and again. Still, uneasy lies the head and all that.

The silence stretched as we both relaxed, although I did the lion's share of relaxing thanks to that heroically comfortable office chair. I waited, he waited, but because he was my friend and I could hardly stand it, I said, "What now?"

"Green Peas."

"Bane of my existence."

"But not mine."

I blinked. "Are you saying what I think you're saying?"

"What am I saying?"

Sigh. "You realize this could go on all day?"

Canton matched my sigh. "I want to train the Green Peas. They need more practice at knife work."

What the—? Ok, step back, Kal, take it in. Take it in. I though. I cogitated and pondered for a minute while Canton sat there like a ruddy marble statue. Something didn't add up, a niggling little detail that felt like a stone in my mental shoe.

Then it hit me. Thanks to years of practice, I kept the realization off my face. "But you want time off first."

Canton's eyes flew wide. Bingo.

So, this was how BB felt when he had my number.

"Yeah, white boy. I need some time off. Visit the parents, my brother and sister. Relax, maybe see the sights."

"Or a certain ninja assassin lady."

There you go. My buddy's face turned a pale shade of red (I won't say pink) and he began to hem and haw and act like a kid who just got caught flogging the dolphin to his daddy's *Playboy* magazine.

"Gotcha!" I crowed, pointing as his face crumpled into unhappy lines. "Gotcha, gotcha, gotcha! You have been well and truly got, my man. You got so got that it's gonna go down in history as one of the world's greatest gots. Oh, yes indeedy. There are gotters out there that will be sooooooo jealous!"

"You done?" Canton's lips barely moved.

"Okay … no … wait. One more …. GOTCHA!" I slumped back. "There. I needed that. I mean, like really, dude, I needed that like breath in my lungs and hope in my heart. I'm married, these little victories keep me sane."

The Apache dared to toss the one raised eyebrow back at me, cheeky monkey. "Should I tell Jeanie that, white boy?"

"Are you out of your damn mind? What, you trying to get me killed?"

My friend began to laugh and a second later I joined him. A few minutes passed while we hee-hawed until our sides felt ready to explode. "Oh, good god and gravy fries," he gasped. "I so needed that."

"You and me both."

A minute later our breaths returned, and we got down to brass tacks. "Okay, buddy, you can have your vacation to hook up with your little assassin chick," I said, leaning back. "Who, as I figure it, somehow got in touch after pulling her disappearing trick. Then you can come back, beat up Green Peas to your heart's content."

"Really?"

Why are people so surprised when I do something nice? I've been known to be nice. I have pictures, even. "Of course. There's no record of this particular Barbara Kahale, she doesn't exist, so I'm not sure if I can really tie her to anything. Especially since I get the sneaking suspicion that you're going to recant any testimony against her should I pursue the matter, right?"

He nodded.

"Right. So, off with ye, go see about a girl and find out if you two have something."

Canton stood, I stood, we hugged. "Thanks, white boy."

"You're welcome. Sometimes it's good to be the king, but Canton ..."

"What?"

"I get wind of her working in the US on anything, and I mean *anything*, illegal and I will come down on her like a metric crap-ton of bricks, you got me?"

"I got you, boss," Canton nodded, and exited stage left.

I pondered the situation I found myself in. Sure, Barbara Kahale was an assassin, but to her credit, I couldn't find a single incident where assassination by a slender young female had ever been recorded. She was *that* good.

But that didn't mean I wouldn't stop looking. I wished my friend some luck.

Now, to business. Thanks to modern magical tech, the normal DRAFT (Data Retrieval And Forensic Tech) glasses had been miniaturized to a set of soft contact lenses that fit me perfectly, one last gift from BB before he pulled his disappearing act. I cleared my throat, activating the lenses.

In my vision there sprung to life a series of icons and I used voice commands to open each file one at a time to catch up on events. I was partway through Team Alpha's encounter on a bug hunt (giant ants in New Mexico) when a flashing red light appeared. I had a call.

"Yes?"

Alex Dumont came into view, occupying the lion's share of my attention. He looked antsy. Or horny ... I could never tell. "Hey kid, what can I do you for?"

"I just read your file, Kal." His face twitched. Definitely horny.

"Good reading. Learn anything?"

"You should be dead."

"Said every bad guy I ever killed."

That earned me an annoyed look. I let it slide off without leaving a slime trail. "You don't understand, Kal, you should be dead. No Magician is able to do what you did with that Zippo spell. *You can't twin a spell!* Every Magician since the dawn of time that has tried to throw two spells at the same time, even easy ones like Zippo, have their brains turned into charcoal briquettes! How did you do that?"

"Talent, kid, sheer talent."

"Kal, really, we have to talk—"

"Sorry kid, gotta go, my manicurist is on line two."

"Kal! Don't you—"

Click.

It's good to be the boss.

Before I could bask in the glory of my own smartitude, another communication icon lit, and I said, "Answer."

Four people appeared, hovering over the desk. It looked spooky as hell. "Oh, Committee members, good to see you. I've been meaning to ring." No, not really. Must work harder on avoiding my *bosses*. I gave the four a good once over.

Admiral Ellison, looking granite hard and about as humorous, Chief Justice Whitehall in her judicial black robe, Senator Stein (D-NE) looking like the politician he was …yuk. Last, but certainly the strangest choice, the Secretary of Education Caroline Brisby. No one knew why POTUS chose her to be on the Committee to oversee the Bureau, but rumor had it she was so smart she could tie her own mind in knots. Prim, proper, short brown hair, she was about as talkative as a brick and that made her all the more dangerous in my book. It was the quiet ones that got you.

Fantastic.

"You should have contacted us earlier, Hakala," said Stein with his legendary gruffness.

"Yeah, but I didn't want to talk to you."

Glowering all around while Stein huffed and puffed like he wanted to blow my house down. Surprise, surprise, it was Brisby who broke the incredulous-ness. "Why not?" she asked in a surprisingly melodic voice.

"Because I have nothing to report at this time and then Senator Stein would get all grumpy and demanding while Admiral Ellison would sit and stare sternly as if he were using some Jedi mind trick while Judge Whitehall would be all judgy and stuff. Frankly, I just don't have time for all the hassle, I've got a lot on my plate and some executively huge shoes to fill here. No, no offense to the committee or anything, but I got crap to do not there's not enough hours in the day."

Brisby's lips twitched. Was that a smile? Nah, must've been hallucinating. Stein, however didn't want to let this one go. He got all politicky on me.

"We can fire you for insubordination, Hakala," he groused, color rising high in his pale cheeks.

"Go ahead." I folded my arms and tried not to smile.

That stopped him cold. Ellison and Whitehall blinked rapidly in confusion while Brisby's tiny smile grew fractionally larger.

"What's going to happen, should you fire my happy ass, is that POTUS will be very unhappy. When I tell the media that I was fired because I needed some time to learn the job, your constituents will be *very* unhappy because, right now, I'm more popular than Beyoncé. When the rest of the Bureau finds out what happened, they will be unhappy, and that will lead to hard times for my replacement."

Quiet. Almost too quiet. Who ever heard of a Beltway committee being quiet for any amount of time? Finally, Ellison broke the silence. "You're being a tad hard on the Senator, son."

That was rich coming from a legendary hardass. "No sir, I'm not."

"Mind telling me why?"

"Because to you and the rest of the Committee I am Director Hakala. Not Hakala, not Kalevi, not *son*. Director Hakala. If you can't show me the courtesy of my station, then you better get off the line, Admiral, because I'm not going to put up with your crap." There. I waited.

Brisby startled everyone by laughing. I think it even must've given God a pause. It was full-throated and rich. It sounded youthful and vibrant. The others stared, as if she'd grown a second head.

When she was done, she winked at me. Winked! I nearly fell off the chair. "Let's leave the Director to the job of running the BSI, shall we. He's absolutely correct, he has a lot of work ahead of him." Her image winked out.

Ellison grunted, and he winked out, too, followed by Whitehall. All that was left was Stein and I and he gave each other the hairy eyeball. "I'm not going to like you, am I?" he asked.

"No. I am a dedicated pain in the ass and I will come at you so hard during appropriation time that you'll think that I have one hand in your wallet and the other in your wife's purse. But I will do my damnedest to be the guy who helps my people survive this job."

A snort and he winked out. I felt a curious sense of victory. It's good to be the boss.

ABOUT THE AUTHOR

CURRENTLY MARK EVERETT STONE lives in California keeping busy with his writing along with the important stuff like being a father and husband. When he's not writing he is carefully keeping an eye on his two cats, who he believes are secret agents sent by an ancient galactic civilization .